WAYWARD PREY

A POST APOCALYPTIC STORY OF SURVIVAL

P.L. SMITH

BOOKS

Published by :
Farmboy Logic Publishing
November 2013

www.plsmithbooks.com

Paperback ISBN: 978-1-940868-00-4
Ebook ISBN: 978-1-940868-02-8

DEDICATION

I would like to thank my supporters wholeheartedly. This book was funded through the Kickstarter organization by some great people who believed in giving a new author a shot. This book is dedicated to them.

Randy & Nancy Smith
Brooke M. Huotte
John & Tina Thomas
Matthew Smith & Dawn Maxson
Sharon & Tony Singleton
Paul Cox
Patricia Guntly & Linda Thompson
Joel Lopez
Rebu, Andy, & Josephine
AMJ
Lori Bock
Diana, Juan, & Lexi
Chad Smith & Jessica Rowe
Rawb Constantine CDe Baca
Samantha Stallcup
Troy Stallcup

Aunt Mary, Uncle Dan, Justin, & Hailey
Kate Platt
Royann Maxson
Reed Maxson
Jim Olson
Robert Griffin
&
All the other supporters that made this dream of mine a reality.

CONTENTS

CHAPTER 1
RUNNING

THE BOY SHIVERED as he watched the sun peek over the horizon. The frost glistened on the leaves of the trees. He brushed the dirt and twigs off his clothes, which had chosen to cling to him instead of the cold ground where he had slept. His body was stiff, his joints cold, and his muscles sore. He could feel the melon-sized bruise above his knee on his right thigh as he walked. He had come a long way yesterday, and the steep terrain had taken its toll on his already damaged body.

He walked down to the creek, rubbing his arms trying to warm himself. Despite the cold, he lay across the rocks and pressed his lips to the stream. He hadn't had any water since he had left home yesterday morning when he had run for his life. It already seemed like an eternity had passed. He drank until his teeth ached and his belly was full. Who knows how long it would be until he found more? He was tattered, hungry, and exhausted.

In his reflection, he could see the dried blood on his face and the darkness of a bruise on his cheekbone. He cupped his hands and splashed the icy water into his face. The chill sent a shock through him that made his skin feel as though tape had been ripped from every inch of his body all at once. He caught his breath and began scrubbing at his crusted face.

At last, satisfied and wanting to escape the chill of the shadowy canyon, he set off, drying his face with his shirt. He had ridden east, on his motorcycle, making it to the foothills before an unseen rock sent him and his dirt bike into the bank. He was forced to run on foot after nearly twenty minutes of trying to kick-start the bike with his now swollen and aching leg. East was the only direction there might be some semblance of safety. Still, he needed to follow the cover of the foothills for as long as possible before he cut across into the exposed deserts and salt flats beyond the Nevada line.

He could try to get supplies in Cedarville and maybe warn them if they hadn't been hit yet. If they had, he would sneak in and steal what he could find. But either way, he was headed for Nevada. He would need some sort of transportation, too. Even a mountain bike would make a difference. He wouldn't last long out in the desert on foot. He had a long way to go and even though the days were still warm, it was fall and the desert nights could be frigid. The faster he could travel, the better off he would be.

His plan was to get to his aunt and uncle's ranch, nestled in a secluded valley in northern Nevada. He spent two weeks there a few years ago, helping on the ranch, back before everything changed. He knew he would be safer there. Besides, there was nothing left for him here. He just hoped they were rural enough that they hadn't been attacked. There were rumors of factions rising up all over; marauders, thieves, and ex-military types attacking towns and stealing fuel, food, supplies, and weapons. Ghost stories, everyone thought. Just ghost stories, until they came. Now his parents were dead, and he was alone.

He had been out in the fields hunting when he heard the shots. They were loud, louder than his old .22 pistol. He figured it was just one of the neighbors plinking around, which he thought was wasteful. All supplies were low in town, especially ammunition. But he listened again, it was too fast to be a semi-auto, someone was shooting with a full-auto weapon. It would have been illegal back in the old days, but now it didn't really matter. Then he heard screams and shots from another direction. He raced back to the house as quickly as he could. It wasn't far, less than a mile from where he was hunting. His mind imagined terrible things, but what he found was worse.

When he reached the yard he stopped, unable to comprehend what he was seeing. He fell to his knees. The heat rushed from his body in an instant. He felt sick. He found them lying near the patio, his father clutching his mother. The blood. His father was still alive. He looked up at him, and could only whisper his name before he died.

Andrew.

Then he heard shouting and more gunshots. Humvees and military trucks full of men raced up and down the road firing at whatever moved. He heard glass breaking and knew someone was in the house. He had his small pistol, but what good would it do? There were dozens of them. He could hear them coming.

Running to the shed he threw open the door, threw his leg over the seat and with one kick his dirt bike roared to life. He sped off, not knowing where he was going, just knew he had to get away. He heard pops behind him and clumps of dirt flew up from the ground at him. He rode his bike down into a dry drainage ditch. It was deep enough to conceal both him and his bike. He followed it all the way to the foothills. He didn't slow down once; he raced as fast as he could away from town, away from his home, and away from his parents. He was scared and he was crying, but he didn't stop, until the wreck.

Andrew leaned against a tree and rubbed his exhausted face. His heart ached at the memory. His vision blurred but he rubbed the tears and pushed the memory aside. He couldn't break down again. His life depended on it. He had to keep moving. As he walked, the muscles in his thighs and calves warmed and loosened, he quickened his pace. He could see Payne Peak; he knew he was close enough that he could make it to Cedarville before nightfall, despite his injured leg. Once he made it to the bottom of the foothills just out of town, he would wait and sneak in after dark in case it had become occupied.

There were no warnings from Cedarville, but then again the weekly mail delivery wouldn't have come until today. It doesn't matter. They hit us fast. There wouldn't have been any way to get a message out. They came from the south but there had been no word of an attack from that direction either, probably no survivors. But Cedarville is in the next valley over. Maybe it's still safe.

As he reached the top of the hill, he glanced back. Smoke on the horizon, lots of smoke. They were burning his town, his home, or what was left of it.

Bastards. Why burn it? Why not take what you need and go? Nothing like the worst tragedy the world has ever seen to bring out all the scumbags of the world. As if the devastation of the disease isn't enough, there have to be pieces of shit left in this world evil enough to steal and murder.

He felt like screaming. If only they had known. If only there had been some kind of warning, they might still be alive.

He trudged on in a daze. Numb to the world around him, numb to the birds, numb to the wind, numb to the swaying grass. He passed a doe within twenty yards and never noticed her. She watched him through black eyes, unmoving. She had been afraid when she first heard him, but waited, not wanting to reveal herself. But as she watched him, nothing about this strange two-legged creature appeared to be a threat. As he passed by she dropped her head back down and continued nibbling the small patch of green grass she had found.

Andrew reached the valley just as the sun was dipping behind him. Across the hay fields, he could see the sleepy little town. No smoke. But that didn't mean anything. He made it to a haystack at the edge of a field and hid there in the bales until the sun had gone down completely. All was silent except the deafening symphony of the crickets. He shivered as the night dew settled in; the smell of wet hay reminded him of the summers past when he had put up hay with his mom and dad.

After the virus diesel had become too scarce to continue farming on a large scale, not that it was needed anyway, and with no power they had no way to turn on their irrigation pumps. Andrew remembered finding his dad standing out in the dry, weedy fields. He had tears in his eyes and he looked broken. The only other time he had ever seen his father cry was when Andrew's grandfather had died.

He told Andrew that all he had ever wanted was to grow this land into something he could pass down to him, to hopefully give him an easier life than he had had. Time went on and they allowed a neighbor to graze his cows on what little did grow in the fields from the winter rains in exchange for meat and they focused on growing vegetables near the house where they could water with their ancient windmill. Things improved and life seemed to resume a small sense of normalcy but that broken look in his father's eyes never went away.

A crow flapped overhead bringing Andrew back from his memory. It was time. He needed to be able to get close enough, without being seen, to be sure that the town wasn't under siege. He steeled himself and began to sneak his way in. It was quiet. He heard nothing, except for a dog barking in the distance. No movement, no lights. Keeping to the shadows he followed one of the back-streets to the general store. It was now nothing more than a marketplace for people to trade. Paper money had become worthless. The only real currency people accepted were silver and gold coins, which were few and far between. Now everything was bartered for. Prices set by the people's need for the items. He had been there a few times with his parents after the collapse. They had brought canned fruit and fresh vegetables from his mother's garden to trade. The thought of his parents put a lump in his throat. He blinked until his eyes cleared again.

Andrew glanced around and quickly ran across the street to the door of the store. It was dark inside, but it wasn't locked. It didn't make sense. Someone should be there. He peered inside. The store was a mess. There were broken jars and bags of food scattered about the floor.

Something's wrong.

He looked around to see that no one was watching him. The town was dead calm and the silence sent a shiver up his back.

There was an old woman who lived in town that his parents knew and visited on occasion. Mrs. Owens. He thought he remembered where she lived, and set off in that direction, doing his best to keep himself concealed. He stopped suddenly. He could hear a car. He ducked behind some bushes just as headlights appeared from around the corner. It was a military-style Humvee, with a spotlight moving back and forth, bathing the street in white light.

So, he was too late. The attackers had already taken over Cedarville too. They had just done a cleaner job this time. Andrew was scared. He didn't know whether to continue to Mrs. Owens or sneak back out of town and make a run for it. She might be dead already, and all her food gone. It was worth the risk he decided. He couldn't go on without supplies. He crept forward; sneaking through yard after yard, until he came upon the house he thought was hers. He made his way around to the back door and decided knocking would attract too much attention. So he tried the doorknob. It turned with a coarse grinding of something not made in this century. He gently pushed the door open, stepping through and pushing it shut, not releasing the knob until the door was tight against the jamb. The floor creaked as he crept through the pantry. He made his way through into the kitchen by the light of the moon shining through the window. As he turned the corner he froze. There, floating in front of him, was a glowing red dot. Then he heard a click. A noise so distinct, it could only be the cocking of a gun. He didn't breathe.

"I may be old, but I can pull a trigger as good as the next one. Keep walking and I'll put you in a pine box."

The voice was hoarse but without anger. Just calm and very matter-of-fact-like.

"Come to steal my food and put a bullet in my head no doubt! Sorry you son of a bitch, I beat you to the punch."

The glowing red dot bobbed up and down with the voice. Then he smelled the familiar scent and remembered. Mrs. Owens had been a smoker.

"Mrs. Owens! It's me! Andrew! You knew my parents. I need help. Don't shoot me!" He was frantic to get his words out before she pulled the trigger. He heard a clunk and a second later saw her hands strike a match. She lit a candle and held it up to his face and then quickly blew it out.

"That was risky, but I had to do it to make sure it was really you. Well, I'll be—little Andrew. I haven't seen you or your parents in ages. What in the hell are you doing here? It's not safe!"

With that, he recounted the last few days' events. He broke down and sobbed when he told her of his parents; having for the first time, someone to share his grief.

"Honey, I'm sorry. It's alright, shhh."

She wrapped her arms around him like he was a child and did her best to console him. After some time he calmed down, exhausted and heartsick.

She told him how after hitting his town, the large group of military-looking men, who called themselves *The Restored Republic*, had come into Cedarville, claiming to impose martial law and that everyone had to turn over their weapons and whatever food they had for stockpiling. Those who refused were shot on the spot. A group of men from the town had attacked the soldiers but were cut down in minutes. The rest of the town was put on house arrest. They were told that anyone found on the streets would be shot. They then planned to go from house to house taking whatever supplies, and whatever else, they wanted.

So Mrs. Owens had decided to load her long-dead husband's double-barrel shotgun and sit and wait.

"If we give up our food, we are as good as dead anyhow." She said. "Might as well take one or two of them out with me!"

Mrs. Owens heated some stew for the boy over her wood stove. He devoured it within minutes. She gave him another helping and then went to the basement. After a time, she returned with a large faded green duffel bag; it had a shoulder strap and drawstring at the top. The kind the military used to use. She dropped it at his feet.

"If you are careful this should be enough food to get you to your aunt and uncle's. This was my husband's coat. It's goose down, you'll need it. Winter's coming. It's just going to keep getting colder. I also put in more bullets for your pistol. Oh! You'll need a sleeping bag."

She dug into the closet and pulled out a bulging stuff sack.

"Alright, follow me."

She led him out through the door into the garage. There in the corner was a dusty Kawasaki KLR 650, the 'doomsday bike', or so it was nicknamed. Andrew remembered when he was younger on one of his parents' visits, coming out and staring at that bike hoping one day to have his own. Mrs.

Owens walked up to the bike and strapped the sleeping bag to the back.

"It was my son's. He rode the hell out of it, but he took care of it. It should run like a dandy. He never came back to get it after he moved to Portland."

She stopped. Andrew could hear the sadness in her voice. She took a deep breath.

"I'd give you my old caddy, but it's pretty well shot. Besides, that bike will go a lot further on less gas. The tank is full and the spare bottles on it are full. You just promise me you won't crack your head open on it!"

Andrew laughed and said that he promised.

"Alright, you go in and get some sleep. I'll wake you before sun up and we'll sneak you out. You'll need to be at least out on the edge of town before you fire this up so they're less apt to hear you. Remember stay on the road for as long as you can but if you see anyone, get off the road and get out of sight. This bike can handle the desert."

Andrew settled into the spare bedroom and dove beneath the covers. It was just an old comforter but as he pulled it over him, it felt like a heavy layer of warmth and safety. He slid his pistol beneath his pillow and felt the reassuring comfort of its grip. His father had given it to him three summers before, on his thirteenth birthday. It had been his grandfather's; even though it was only a .22 it was designed to look like a German Luger from World War II. It was old but it had been cared for and Andrew had become quite skilled with it. It had made him feel like a man when his dad had given it to him. Now it was all he had left.

―――――

Andrew awoke in a cold sweat. He had relived the death of his parents in a nightmare, only it had been worse, much worse. He didn't think that could be possible, but it was. A noise had brought him out of the hellish nightmare. He tried to calm his heartbeat and listen. There it was again, a pop. Someone was shooting, not very far away either. The door to his room burst open and in ran Mrs. Owens.

"Change of plans, kiddo. You're going to have to hit the road sooner than we thought. Those no-good sons of bitches are next door at the Kensington's, and someone is shooting. I've gotta get over there and help them. You get on that bike and you ride for your aunt and uncle's! Don't trust anyone. Keep out of sight and you'll get there. I put a map in your bag too. You'll probably need it. Get your things and get going. I have got to run. Good luck son."

"Wait, I can help..."

"No! The only thing you need to do is get to your aunt and uncle's. Don't worry about the noise, just start it and go. There should be enough commotion; they won't notice you until you are on your way out of town. No matter what you hear just keep going, don't stop 'til you're past the state line. Good luck and God bless you, Andrew. Now get!"

The old woman ran out of the room clutching the enormous shotgun. With his coat on, Andrew grabbed his pistol and the duffel bag of food and ran for the garage. He strapped the duffel bag over his shoulder and shoved the pistol into its holster at his belt. He threw his leg over the dusty bike and with a shock of fear, he realized his feet could barely touch the ground. This bike was much bigger than what he was used to. He threw his shoulder back to shift the duffel bag more squarely on his back. He turned the key on, set the choke, squeezed the clutch, and punched the ignition with his thumb. He held his breath. The engine turned over but made no sign of firing. He tried it again. Nothing. His heart sank. He played with the choke. Still nothing. Mrs. Owens had left the garage door wide open for him to get out. He could see men running back and forth in the darkness. Soon they'd notice him, and soon he'd be full of bullet holes.

He was frantic. He decided to just make a run for it. Then he remembered the fuel shutoff valve and felt like slapping himself in the forehead. He reached down the side of the tank, next to his knee, and felt it. He turned the valve, pointing it straight down. He hit the ignition again. The engine cranked. Once. Twice. On the third turn, the engine fired awake. He throttled with his wrist and dust blew out of the exhaust pipe. He threw up his kickstand and flipped on his headlight.

There bathed in the light, directly in front of him was a man, dressed in tactical gear, carrying an assault rifle. The man was blinded by the light, but he began to swing the gun towards him. Andrew squeezed the clutch, kicked down into first, and gunned the bike. His rear tire slid sideways on the slick concrete; then the bike righted itself and whipped so hard he nearly lost his balance.

Andrew drove straight for the man. A flash and then pain seared at his arm; it felt like it was on fire. The man dove out of the way just before the bike hit him. Andrew screamed out in pain and nearly lost control of the bike when he hit the street, but he stayed on the throttle and leaned his body to make the turn. He lifted the gear shift up into second and gunned it. The pain in his arm blazed again when he squeezed the clutch to shift.

One more turn, then straight out of town.

He slowed a bit and leaned into the turn. Out of the corner of his eye, he saw an eruption of muzzle flashes. The bullets showered sparks across the pavement, the man firing wildly. Andrew made it around the corner, behind the next house, and was out of sight, safe from the gunfire for the moment.

Andrew let off the throttle and shifted up, this time without the clutch, and sped off into the darkness. He laid his arm across his stomach and rested it there. It was throbbing with pain. He could feel warm sticky blood all the way down his arm to the cuff of his jacket. His head was swimming. He knew he needed to stop the bleeding. But he had to go as far as he could; he knew they'd be coming after him.

Just a few more miles and he'd be into Nevada, and the desert beyond. From there, once he crossed the small range of hills, he knew the dirt roads spider-webbed out. In the dark, his pursuers would have no idea which way he went. He could find a place to hide and check on his arm.

Twice his eyelids got too heavy to hold up and he veered onto the rumble strips. But when his eyes snapped open, his conscious mind shut down and his instincts took over, saving him from a spill. He had had a lot of practice in the sand and mud with his little dirt bike. Riding had become as comfortable as walking to him, as though the wheels were extensions of his legs.

His eyes drooped once more, and this time he opened them to the sight of headlights in his mirror. He quickly veered to the right and took a side road that looked rough and seldom used, careful not to touch his brakes. The dust might conceal the glow of his headlight but a red brake light is made to be seen.

The terrain was still hilly enough that he was able to find a small ravine to hide in. He idled the bike down into the ravine and stopped on a flat area near a rock that he was sure wouldn't be seen from the road.

He waited, listening. He heard the vehicle get nearer and then drifted further away. They must not have seen him. He let out his breath, safe for the moment. He put down his kickstand and did his best to drag himself off the tall bike without falling over, the weight of his bag nearly toppling him. At the point of exhaustion, Andrew dropped the large sack and collapsed at the base of the rock to rest for a moment before dealing with his arm. He exhaled, trying to slow his breathing. His body and his mind felt equally heavy.

How did it all come to this?

They knew so little about the virus. It was a new strain

that scientists had never seen, it was a serious problem but after the COVID-19 epidemic, no one was panicking, after all, the virus was only dangerous to animals. In the beginning, the outbreaks were limited to factory farms, and mass-production livestock facilities raising cattle, swine, and poultry.

The first report was like a horror story. Some poultry farmer in the Midwest woke up one morning and headed to his first barn, a massive sealed steel warehouse, devoid of light. It was an open floor, cage-free type facility. Andrew remembered seeing it on the news. Thousands upon thousands of dead, lifeless chickens were scattered across the floor of the warehouse. The farmer had run then to each of his other seventeen flinging open the doors. When he saw the motionless carcasses of the final warehouse, he collapsed. At least that's what the blond news reporter had relayed as the camera panned back and forth over the sea of decaying birds.

Two other poultry facilities and a swine processing plant were infected within a day. Within a couple of weeks, livestock facilities across the country had been hit. Footage shot from helicopters showed miles and miles of feedlots filled with bloated cattle carcasses. The USDA and the CDC did everything they could to control it, but by the time they arrived to shut down one infected plant, five more reported dead livestock. A 'No Transport' quarantine was put into effect; not one piece of livestock was allowed to move in the United States. But it was too late; within a month every large-scale farm or processing plant had been infected and shut down. The stench of death rode upon the wind as panic set in.

Supermarkets pulled every type of meat from their shelves. Food shortages ensued as people bought whatever vegetables and canned goods they could. Riots had begun to break out, first in the densely populated cities, then in the smaller, suburban areas. Everyone thought that things couldn't get any worse. Then the virus made the jump.

The first human casualties were along the grain belt of the Midwest, the same area where the virus originated, Iowa and Nebraska; then Ohio, Kansas and South Dakota. At first, the media did everything they could to dissuade the idea that the virus and the human infection were the same, hoping to stave off the panic. But as the bodies stacked up, people knew the truth. Finally, the President and the CDC made the announcement. The other leaders of the world did the same. All flights were grounded. For the first time in a century, other than patrolling military jets, not one plane left the ground in the entire civilized world. Action, once again taken too late, the virus erupted across Europe and Asia. Panic swept across the planet.

Andrew remembered sitting in the living room with his parents watching when the President gave his speech. He had said that everyone should remain calm and stay in their homes. The world's top scientists were working on a vaccine, and he was working with the UN Council taking inventory of the world's food supply. He had said that there was more than enough to go around and that we must come together as a country, to support one another; to not hoard supplies, causing further shortages.

After his speech, the news anchor came back to announce the current U.S. death toll. At that point, it was estimated at five hundred thousand. As a side story, scientists were puzzled as to why so few livestock deaths had been reported in areas where the animals were raised on pastures instead of feedlots. They theorized that it was because most of these areas were secluded and cut off from major transit lines. However, it was later discovered that these animals were immune to the virus.

They were also beginning to find humans that were immune as well, carrying a built-in genetic resistance; as if our ancestors had seen this strain before. Scientists did everything they could to synthesize antibodies, but it was too little too late. Within six months the world as the 21st century knew it, was over. The government had collapsed and the last reported death toll, before the power went out, was one hundred million in the U.S. alone.

Andrew shuddered when he remembered what it felt like when they lost power and communication. The virus had already come and gone through their sleepy little farm town in northern California. It had taken its toll but it was nothing compared to the percentages of deaths in other areas. The town had an unusually high immunity rate but had still lost fifty-six of its eighty-three inhabitants. A gloom had settled over the little town. No one left their houses unless they had to, and everyone did their best to avoid contact with others.

Six months later things had begun to settle. People began to enjoy life again. Even though power and electronic communication had shut down, the surrounding towns had re-established a mail route with each other. Fuel was becoming scarce, so deliveries were made on motorcycles instead of cars because they were more efficient. The shorter routes were even made on horseback. Life returned to a near facsimile of normal. People were forced to learn how to make things and grow things again. Those who were proficient at one craft traded their wares for what they needed. Markets were set up where people could bring their goods to trade. People learned how to survive again.

Andrew had taken to hunting for cotton-tails in the over-grown alfalfa fields. Although he didn't care for the taste, there were those in town who did and gladly traded for them. He had spotted one running from the brush and was about to fire when he heard the shots and then the screams. The horrible screams.

CHAPTER 2
NO REST FOR THE HUNTED

ANDREW WOKE with the sound of tires crunching gravel. With a start, he sat up. He looked around wildly. It was light, for how long he didn't know. The sky was gray and overcast. He crawled on his belly up until he could see the road. All he saw was a cloud of dust speeding away. He had done well finding this spot. They'd have to be searching on foot to stumble upon the small ravine.

As he crawled back to his bag, he felt the pain in his arm when he moved and remembered he hadn't taken care of his wound before he fell asleep. His lips were dry and cracked, and his mouth was so parched he felt like he couldn't swallow. He found a bottle of water in the duffel bag and drank nearly half of it without taking a breath. The bottle wobbled as he set it down into the sand, gasping for breath, the need for water temporarily outweighing the need for air.

Looking down, he decided the coat had to come off. He started working it off at the cuff, pulling and peeling at the sleeve. He had to reach inside his coat to peel the sleeve away from the wound. It hurt and he could feel it start to bleed again. Finally, his arm slipped free.

The wound wasn't as bad as he had thought. The bullet

must have just grazed him. Although it had gotten close enough to take a three-inch long, quarter-inch deep gouge out of his bicep, luckily it hadn't hit the bone. He looked closer and could see a piece of material from his jacket still in the wound, trapped in the dried blood and tissue. He knew he had to get it out and then clean the wound as best he could to keep from getting an infection. He pulled out a blue handkerchief; he carried it out of habit, in his back pocket just like his dad had. He poured a little water on it, careful to not waste too much. Then he held the wet cloth to his arm until the dried blood began to soften. He carefully wiped at the blood, then slowly peeled out the scrap of material. It hurt and he could feel it tearing the scabs that had formed beneath it. When it was free, he could feel the wound oozing blood.

Blood dripped to the sand as he poured water down his arm. He did his best to clean the wound with the handkerchief and then dug into the bag again for some sort of dressing and discovered a clean pair of socks.

Good old Mrs. Owens.

He wrung out his handkerchief and laid it on his knee. He took one of the socks, wadded it up, and pressed it against his wound. It hurt but it felt good to know it was bandaged. The sock may not be sterile but his wound would be as clean and protected as he could make it. He took his handkerchief, wrapped it around his arm, and tied it over the top of the sock using his teeth and his free hand. When the knot was tied he let out a deep breath.

Now what?

The answer came almost instantly.

Food.

Mrs. Owens' stew had been the last thing he had eaten. He wasn't sure what time it was but he was positive he had missed at least one meal. He dug into his bag and found a jar of canned pears. He opened it up, ate the entire contents, and then drank the juice, thinking it had to be the best thing he had ever tasted. He licked the sticky juice from his fingers, put the lid back on the jar, and stowed it in his bag. He slid his coat back on and was glad of its warmth. His sleeve was stiff and crusted from the blood. Goose feathers peeked out through the torn bullet hole.

Way to ruin a perfectly good coat.

He crept to the top of the ravine and glanced around. He could still see the dust cloud but it was miles away now. The panorama of the desert was painted with the bleakness of autumn. He decided if he went slow at first and didn't kick up too much dust he could put some more distance between him and his attackers, *The Restored Republic.*

He drank some more water and stowed the bottle back in the bag. The pain in his abdomen told him he needed to relieve himself before he got back on the bike. When he was done, he threw the bag across his shoulders and kicked his leg across the seat of the bike, the tips of his toes barely keeping the bike from falling over. He fired up the engine and let it idle for a moment, giving the oil time to work its way through the motor.

The gash beneath the cotton sock stretched as he squeezed the clutch in and out. His arm hurt, but he could stand it, he'd need full control of his hand to feather the clutch to get out of this little ravine. The bike lurched forward an inch as he kicked down into first gear. The clutch handle eased out as he opened his hand and the bike crept forward as he slowly made his way out. Within minutes he was back on the rough little dirt road. It felt good to be back on the bike and moving again. With each mile, he felt closer to safety, even though he had no idea where it was.

The cool air numbed his ears and stung his nostrils. He leaned his head from shoulder to shoulder trying to warm his ears. For the first time, he wished he had a helmet. His mom always insisted he wear his when he went riding, but as soon as he would meet up with his friends, he'd tear it off and strap it to the back of his bike.

After a couple of hours of fighting ruts, ditches, and washboards, it struck him that the road he was on could be taking him in the completely wrong direction. He decided to check his map. The bike came to a stop as he made it to the top of a small hill. It was a good vantage point for spotting landmarks and he could easily see if anyone was coming. He parked the bike, hauled his duffel over to the top of the bluff, and sat down. He breathed in the cool desert air. It was almost cold enough to see his breath.

There was something about the desert that had always drawn him. The vast landscape that disguised itself as an empty wasteland, but to those who knew it, it revealed its secrets. Stretched out in front of him was what looked like miles of flat desert, a sea of rippling dust broken up by patches of sagebrush. But he knew better; a person could start walking and within minutes be completely hidden from sight. The desert was like that, a honeycomb of dry river beds, canyons, and gullies, all hidden in plain sight, all of them hiding secrets of their own.

To his north, he could see a range of low mountains, with a lone peak at the tail. The only landmarks on his map that were similar to what he was seeing were a pair of small ranges, one called Badger Mountain and one Nut Mountain.

People come up with some strange names.

He didn't know which he was looking at. Badger or Nut, either way, he was much further south than he wanted to be; and the road he was on wasn't on the map as far as he could tell. That was the problem with back roads, there were so many of them crisscrossing back and forth, that it was impossible to know if you were on the right one. Most were simply bike or jeep trails. He had passed at least four intersections in just the last hour. Some roads were in a little better shape and some were much worse. He traced a route on the map with his finger, from his guessed location. If he stayed heading east, he'd reach the salt flats of the Black Rock Desert and he could follow those north, up into the farming country. He knew his uncle's ranch was in one of the valleys to the north, but most of the valleys on the map weren't named. Frustrated, he tossed the map back into the bag.

The sky was darkening. He had slept later than he thought. As the sun was beginning to set, the horizon lit up with the most brilliant shades of pink, purple, and blue he had ever seen. He sat and watched the colors dance across the sky and fade into a darkening red. He snapped out of his gazing and realized he needed to find a place to camp soon, no point in driving at night anymore. If the road changed direction, he might not realize it. He didn't want to be any more lost than he was and despite sleeping so much this morning, he was feeling drained.

He found an outcrop of rocks at the bottom of a small cliff descending the bluff. The rock was on the opposite side of the road, keeping him hidden even if someone drove by. It would have to do. He found a spot where the rocks made sort of a dish. At least he could sleep with his back to it and position his bike to the side. It would form a bit of a windbreak and a small barrier against whatever might be lurking out in the night. It would be more of a mental comfort than actual physical protection. He was used to camping out, occasionally alone, but something about his plight and the fact that his parents were no longer there to protect him made him feel vulnerable, more than ever.

He unstrapped his sleeping bag and pulled it from the stuff sack, positioning the head of the mummy bag against the rock, next to the rear wheel of the bike. He had backed the bike up to the rock; so that if need be, he could jump on and make a speedy departure. After untying the handkerchief from his arm, he carefully peeled away the sock which was more red than white. But he was pleased to see the wound was no longer bleeding. He retrieved the clean sock from the bag and bandaged himself back up.

The bloody sock flew through the air as he threw it, landing in the branches of a distant sagebrush. He didn't want the smell of blood attracting any unwanted visitors to his campsite while he slept. Rumors of wolves spreading further south into the area worked away at his imagination. His hand unconsciously touched the grip of his pistol.

He collected as much dry sagebrush as he could find to build a fire. It would serve as a barrier on his only exposed side. It was a risk, but being this far from any of the main roads, and being tucked into the side of the bluff, he felt it was an acceptable one. He dropped the last load onto his sizable pile just as darkness was setting in. He used a flat rock to scoop out a bowl into the ground. When it was about two feet across and eight inches deep in the middle he tossed the rock aside and set about building a pyramid with the dry sticks. He leaned them against one another forming a miniature tepee. He left enough room to deposit a wad of dry grass he had found and a few of the smaller sticks underneath. As he was putting on the finishing touches he heard a growl. It had come from his stomach. He snorted and decided a meal was in order.

He sat down on his sleeping bag and began feeling around in his duffel bag. He found a peel-top can of Crown Prince smoked sardines. He ate them and while licking the greasy oil from his fingers, he thought that food must taste better when you're really hungry because he didn't remember canned fish ever tasting this good. He smiled and looked up at the sky. There was a break in the clouds and he could see a patch of stars shining through the clear cold air. He decided he was being silly and that a fire would just attract attention. It would be a long shot, but out here the glow of a fire can be seen from a long way away, and if his pursuers were still after him there was a chance they would spot the glow.

He stood and tossed the empty sardine can as far as he could. He would look in the morning and pick it up if he found it, but for tonight he wanted it away from where he would be sleeping. He nestled down into his sleeping bag and draped his coat over the top half of the bag, it would add extra insulation and if need be he could pull it over the top of his head if he got too cold.

He drifted off to sleep remembering the last time he had gone camping with his dad. It was the same summer he had given him the pistol. They had taken the canoe for a fishing trip to Fallen Leaf Lake just south of Tahoe. His dad had almost tipped the boat when Andrew hooked a big trout because he was so excited. He remembered his dad taking what seemed like a thousand pictures of him and his fish. He showed him how to gut it and clean it, and after wrapping it in foil with butter and garlic, they tossed the whole thing onto the coals of the fire. It was the most fun he had ever had and the best fish he had ever eaten.

———

Andrew awoke, sitting straight up in his bag, his hands scrambling for his pistol. A noise had torn him from his sleep. He had never heard it before except on TV, but it was unmistakable. It was a mountain lion cry and it was close. The blood was pounding in his ears and he had trouble remembering where he was.

The safety clicked as he slid it down with his thumb and aimed his pistol into the darkness. He pointed it up into the air but in the direction, he thought the cougar was and fired, once then twice more quickly. He stumbled up, kicking out of his sleeping bag, and flipped on the headlight of his bike, illuminating the darkness. Nothing moved. The shots should have been enough to scare anything off, but he decided that a fire was once again worth the risk. One shaking hand dug into the bag to find the matches, while the other held the trembling pistol, keeping at bay the ghosts of the night.

Finally, his fingers closed on a box of matches. He glanced around again, saw nothing, and knelt down, laying his pistol next to him. He worked open the box of matches as quickly as he could, feeling every hair on his body standing on end. He struck the match and the igniting phosphorus burst the end of the match into a glowing yellow flame. A sudden small gust snuffed it out. The extinguished match fell to the ground and he scrambled for another one. He struck it and this time he held his hand to it and guided it to the small cup of dry grass tinder he had formed. The grass cracked and popped as it lit and burned. It spread quickly and began torching the sagebrush twigs above it. The smell of the smoke rising up hit his nostrils, and as the light of the fire spread, a wave of relief swept over Andrew.

He picked up his pistol and sat back against the rock. The fire burned to his left, the bike sat to the right, and the pistol rested firmly in his grip. He felt safer but doubted he'd ever be able to sleep again. As soon as coals would start to form, he would feed the fire and build it back up again. He was determined to stay awake to feed the fire and make sure the cat didn't come back. But after about an hour of peering back and forth from the darkness and then into the dancing flames, his eyelids felt like lead weights. With his head back against the rock, the goose-down jacket draped over him, and the old pistol dozing in his lap, he slept.

CHAPTER 3
HANGING FROM RAFTERS

HE WOKE to light raindrops landing on his face. The raindrops formed little dimples in the powder of the warm ash of his burned-out fire. The sun was up but the thick clouds blocked out most of the light. It was a warm rain for this time of year. He guessed the temperature to be in the mid-fifties, maybe even sixties. The thick low clouds trapped the warmth of the earth, just like the sleeping bag he was curled up inside trapped the warmth of his body.

Andrew breathed in the light breeze and the smell of wet sage filled his nostrils and awakened his senses. There was something about the desert when it rained; it was as though all life stood still to soak up the miracle of the life-giving water.

He sat up against the rock with his jacket over his head and watched a veil of gray rain move slowly across the valley in front of him. Andrew twisted, stretching his back, kneading the knots that had formed over rocks beneath his sleeping bag. He very much missed his soft bed and his warm home.

The breeze picked up, blowing in his face. Suddenly he realized the gray wall of rain was moving towards him. The heavy drops belted down on his makeshift shelter. Knowing there was no point in going anywhere he decided he'd use the time to take inventory of his food supply. One by one he pulled each item out of his duffel and stacked it neatly on a flat rock next to him. He felt like a rich man.

All in all, he had five more cans of sardines, two large bags of dehydrated fruit, two bags of jerky, three apples, and a two-liter bottle of water beside the one he was drinking, which was about half full. He celebrated by eating an apple; he knew they would spoil first, long before any of the other items.

His empty stomach growled as his tongue tasted the sweet fruit. He ravenously ate everything but the stem. Then he tried a couple of pieces of the jerky. It was venison, young and tender, and with lots of spices. He sighed in pleasure, savoring the rich saltiness of the dried meat, and decided to have another.

When the rain stopped, he packed everything back into his bag. The rain beaded off his coat as he shook it and he slipped his arms back inside it again. The duffel bag strap came up over his head and rested on his shoulders, only this time the weight of it didn't bear him down. The weight of it felt like riches, a wealth that would see him through to safety.

He swung his leg over the seat of the bike and shimmied up. After he let the engine warm up for a bit, he kicked it into gear and started out slow, getting a feel for how the bike handled the now slick desert mud. It handled nothing like his old bike. Besides being four times the size, it was much more top-heavy. He had to be alert and on edge constantly. The rear tire fish-tailed and threatened to send him flying multiple times. He rode with his feet out, ready to provide support if he started to lose his balance.

At a bend in the road, he crept through too slow and the bike began to fall and the rear tire slid out from under him. His leg came out to catch the ground but as he did so his hand slipped on the throttle, revving the motor. The back tire slid faster and slammed the bike down on its side. The force knocked him back, landing squarely on his butt in the muddy road. With a surge of adrenaline, he leaped to his feet and hit the switch to kill the motor.

Still shaking, he did his best to brush the mud off his pants and seemed to only smear it around more. Frustrated, he gave up and checked the condition of the bike. It looked alright but he'd have to get it stood back up before he could be sure. He pushed the kickstand down on the opposite side so that it would catch itself when he stood it up.

Finding a dry spot, he laid his bag down at the foot of a large sagebrush. The muddy road sucked at his shoes as he walked back to the bike and positioned himself. Grabbing the handlebars, he lifted. It was heavy, heavier than he thought it would be. He had it halfway up when his feet started to slip. He could feel the wound on his bicep stretching and the scab tearing. He tried to dig in but he just couldn't get a hold with his feet. Finally, he had to drop it back down. Twice more he tried with the same result. His chest was heaving and he was covered from the waist down in the sticky mud.

The sock shifted a bit as he peeked at his wound. It hadn't bled much. He stared at the bike trying to decide what to do. If he couldn't get it back on its wheels he would have to abandon the bike and go on foot. The idea of walking didn't appeal to him very much; he knew he was still well over a hundred miles from his uncle's ranch.

He thought about trying to rig up a lever of some kind with a couple of pieces of wood, but as he surveyed his surroundings he realized that wasn't going to happen. The only things growing out here were sagebrush, and their branches were short and flimsy.

His body grew tense, feeling the need for haste. He was a sitting duck out in the open. There was a hope that his pursuers had given up. After all, what would be the point of continuing the chase? Surely whatever supplies they thought he was carrying couldn't be worth the effort it would take to go after him, but there was still a chance. Desperate people do desperate things. Regardless the rain had made it easy for anyone happening along to follow his tracks. His eyes continuously darted to the top of the hill behind him where the road disappeared.

Think Andrew, think.

Walking around the bike a few times, he noted that the bike was only about five feet from the edge of the road where it dropped off into a small ditch. It might just give him an advantage if he could just drag the bike into the ditch. It would be muddier there to get going if he did get it up but he'd worry about that when the time came.

He worked the bike closer and closer to the ditch, pulling at one tire and then the other. It was slow going and at times it seemed like he was just seesawing the bike back and forth. Finally, his back aching and his body drenched in sweat, he thought that it might be far enough. He took the bottle of water from his bag and drank what was left without a breath. Stowing it back in his bag, a thought came to him.

He set about picking up dead sagebrush branches. Dropping them next to the bike and stomping them into the mud, he formed a mat to stand on. Ready to try again, he positioned himself and lifted. The angle helped him lift a little further this time and his feet held thanks to the traction of the makeshift mat.

His muscles strained as he lifted the bike, this time high enough that he was able to slip his knee under the gas tank and support some of the weight there. He sucked in a deep breath and pushed with all the strength he could muster. As the bike reached its center of gravity, he exhaled, his lungs and muscles burning. He had to lean back and pull to keep the bike from falling too quickly in the other direction in case the kickstand didn't hold in the mud. He let out a sigh of relief when he felt it take over the weight and the bike stood.

While stretching the tension from his back, he examined the mud-caked side of the bike. The drop had cracked the plastic fairing covering the gas tank. Not a big deal, but it would probably flap like crazy in the wind if he ever got back on a highway. He took a small stick and scraped the mud off as best he could around the chain and the hubs. He pushed a big chunk of mud off the footrest and noticed that the foot brake was bent. He thought it should still be usable, just might be a little trickier to feel with his foot, but he still had his hand brake. All in all not a terrible fall and it could have been worse.

As the sun broke through the clouds he looked up and could feel its warmth on his face, it felt good. His muscles quivered from the exertion but the appearance of the sun filled him with a sense of hope. With a bit of a spring in his step, he grabbed his bag, threw it over his shoulders, and tightened the strap. Standing on the high side he was able to easily throw his leg over and mount the bike. Turning the key, he held his breath and, with his thumb, he punched the starter. It cranked over for a few seconds and then roared to life. He smiled.

Bulletproof.

The sun glistened brightly on all the little puddles in the road. As he made his way carefully out of the little valley and up into the foothills, he was relieved to see that the farther he went the better the roads got. Topping a hill he could see a glistening body of water far off in the distance. He decided to try to make it there tonight and camp. If he could locate it on his map he'd know exactly how far off course he had gotten. With a little luck, he'd be riding into his aunt and uncle's by tomorrow.

———

The sun was just setting when he reached the reservoir. He was tired and his butt and back were sore. As he topped a small hill overlooking the water he grabbed the brakes, skidded to a stop, and froze. There below him next to the water was an Army-green, mud-spattered Humvee.

Stashing his bike behind the small hill, he belly-crawled back to the top. He could see the Humvee was actually parked next to a small cabin; he couldn't see anyone and assumed they must all be inside. There was a chance it wasn't his pursuers but what were the odds of that? For a moment he thought he could hear voices inside the cabin. He sat waiting for a few minutes and then decided to push his bike as far back as he could before firing it up and then hightailing it out of there.

No point in sticking around.

Just as he was about to get up he heard the crunch of a boot behind him. He turned and went for his pistol, but it was too late; he saw the butt of a rifle, and a shower of lights exploded across his vision, and then--darkness.

———

When Andrew opened his eyes he could make little sense of what he was seeing; ahead of him was a dancing figure of light. It was bending in on itself, twisting and contorting in the darkness. He blinked, trying to make sense of it. His eyes blurred and then cleared again. The dancing light was calling to him, ushering him to follow. The being of light was rippling now, like water. He looked up and realized he had been staring at the reflection of the moon on a body of water, like a small lake.

It all rushed back to him. Andrew could feel where the blow had landed on the side of his face when he wiggled his jaw. It was throbbing but he didn't think anything was broken. He suddenly realized his hands were above him. He was hanging from the porch rafters of the little cabin. He twisted his wrists and felt the rope dig into his tingling hands.

"Well, it looks like our little buddy is awake," came a voice from his right.

Andrew twisted and in the fading light, he could see a tall man wearing a black padded vest and khakis, carrying a rifle. He had a strong-looking face, high cheekbones, and a defined jawline. He gave Andrew a friendly smile.

"How's the cheek? Sorry about that, Jack doesn't do much thinking before he acts. He's practically worthless. Here, you're probably thirsty."

A canteen appeared in front of Andrew and he drank.

"That's good, not too much now. You don't want to make yourself sick; you have got to be careful after a blow to the head like that. So, what's your name kid?"

"Andrew," he answered, his head swimming.

"Come on, Commander. We don't have time for this shit."

Andrew noticed for the first time two other men standing near the Humvee, watching.

"Shut up! Go do something useful Jack, collect some firewood or something!"

"This is the desert! There is no freaking wood!"

"Do as you're ordered!" snapped the Commander.

Jack sauntered off into the darkness without another word.

"It's not easy leading men, especially when they're degenerates like Jack there. No respect. No proper training whatsoever. Anyhow. That's a nice bike you got there, perfect for this kind of country. Looks like you banged it up a little. Lucky. People don't walk away from many motorcycle wrecks. Looks to be just cosmetic though. My daddy always said 'It's not the chrome that wins the race!'."

The Commander chuckled.

"You know kid, we could use someone like you in our ranks; young, resourceful, tough. You'd fit right in. We do a lot of traveling, but you'd have every need met. It's not a bad life. We're starting over, rebuilding this country. That's why we call ourselves 'The Restored Republic'."

"You're murderers," said Andrew flatly.

The Commander continued without seeming to notice.

"Yup, not a bad life. We just left Lake Tahoe last week. Beautiful. All those big mansions abandoned, we lived like kings right on the shore. Thinking about heading back there as soon as we finish our supply run, maybe even do some skiing. I think you'd like it, but if you've got somewhere else you're headed, I understand."

Andrew almost agreed to go. The Commander had that effect. He almost made Andrew forget that he was part of the group that killed his parents; might have even been him that pulled the trigger and that he was hanging by his bleeding wrists from a rafter.

"Where were you headed, by the way? Maybe we could help you get there. If they have got supplies we could do some trading. We are running low on dry goods and such."

Andrew glared in the Commander's eyes and spat.

"Go to hell! You killed my parents!"

"I see. Well, don't say I didn't offer. Now we have to do it the hard way."

He backhanded Andrew so hard that the rafter above groaned from the force.

"Alright, Lamar. You're up."

"Finally, some fun!"

It was the first time the other man had spoken. He was a hulk of a man clad in camouflage cargo pants. His tattooed torso, chest, and shoulders were bare except for his unzipped tactical vest. As he approached, he pulled a grizzly-looking knife from his belt.

"Alright Lamar, find out what we need to know. He had to be going somewhere."

The Commander disappeared into the cabin and returned

with a glowing lantern. He hung it from a hook on one of the porch post beams and sat in a rocking chair on the far side of the porch. He pulled a small knife from his pocket and began cleaning his fingernails with the tip of the blade.

"You know you gave us quite a chase. We drove all over this damn desert looking for you, kid. Bouncing around in that damned Humvee. My back is killing me thanks to you."

As Lamar spoke he cut Andrew's shirt off in pieces, his razor of a knife slicing easily through the cotton tee letting it drop to the floor. The cold blade sent a shiver through Andrew as he placed it on his collarbone, next to his neck. His heart hammered, and his fear caught in his lungs.

Lamar drug the point down lightly at first and Andrew winced as he felt the sting as the blade barely sliced through his skin leaving a thin line of blood. All at once Lamar sliced diagonally through his chest, cutting deeply. Andrew screamed out. Tears ran freely down his face as the blood oozed down his abdomen. The pain was worse than anything he had ever felt.

"Well kid, are you gonna tell us what we need to know?"

Lamar picked up one of the shirt scraps and nonchalantly wiped the blood from his blade.

Andrew grit his teeth and spat through the tears.

"You're just going to kill me."

"Listen, kid, we may be rough, but we're not blood-thirsty killers. We aren't the ones that killed your parents. That was probably a different unit. The Commander meant what he said about you joining us. Think about it, plenty of food, a warm bed at night. All you gotta do is tell us where you are going. How is that a bad deal?"

"No."

Andrew was feeling dizzy again and couldn't muster any other act of defiance other than the one word.

"Lamar, do something that will let him know that you're serious. The night is beginning to take on a chill."

The Commander spoke as if he were telling his children to clean up their toys because it was getting late. Lamar's blade sliced through the rope and he had to catch Andrew as he fell. He grasped the rope still around Andrew's wrists and jerked him over to the porch railing. Taking a hold of the little finger on Andrew's right hand he pulled it over the edge of the porch rail. Andrew's eyes grew wide.

"No!"

Andrew bucked and struggled but before he could pull away, the knife hacked. Andrew heard a blood-curdling scream and realized it was him. He fell back onto the floor of the porch. His hand curled into as tight a fist as he could make, trying to squeeze out the pain. His vision darkened and his skin felt hot and tingly. He stared in disbelief at the little stump pumping blood down his arm. He vomited then, with the world spinning around him.

A commotion in the darkness caused the Commander to spring to his feet. Lamar turned and looked trying to spot what had made the noise.

"Jack?," yelled the Commander. "Answer me you son of a bitch!"

Silence.

"Jack, is that you? Jack?!"

In his daze, Andrew thought the Commander sounded scared, but then again he wasn't entirely sure what reality was at this point.

"Kill him, Lamar, we're leaving."

Lamar turned back to Andrew. He tried to move, tried to crawl away, but his body was frozen as the mass of Lamar squatted down in front of him.

"Sorry kid."

Andrew watched in horror as the blade pierced his side, sliding between his ribs. He cried out. It felt like a hot iron sliding inside him. It felt so unnatural that every muscle in his body convulsed, trying to expel the foreign object.

Suddenly a shower of crimson erupted from Lamar's neck, which Andrew couldn't explain. All he could think was how strange it was for something like that to come out of someone's neck. He felt the knife leave his rib cage, and then he felt a warmth spreading down his side. It was nice; the rest of him was very cold.

I should get my blanket, he thought.

He felt tired and slowly allowed himself to slump down onto the deck.

He heard pops.

Who would be making popcorn out here? I'll have a nap first, just a little nap.

Andrew let the darkness take him.

CHAPTER 4
EMPTY TRAPS

LEE WAS NERVOUS. He didn't usually get nervous, being an experienced trapper, hunter, and all-around outdoorsman for the better part of his sixty-odd years. He had been stalked before by cats, and even a grizzly up in the waist-deep snow of northern Idaho. That ended up being a close one, but even then he had never felt hunted. He felt it now.

He scratched the thick matted beard at his chin and then the smooth bald skin under his old knit cap. He didn't have much experience with wolves. They had been around back in his days of trapping up in the north; Idaho, Montana, and even parts of British Columbia. But in those days they were few and far between. You were damned lucky to see one within a couple of miles; elusive to say the least. Then by the time the government started planting them, increasing their numbers, and forcing their expansion into southern Idaho, Oregon, and even portions of Northern California, Lee had since moved south and started his guiding service in the never-ending mountains of Nevada.

Coyotes were abundant out here. But this was different. He had never had a coyote smart enough to take bait from a trap without tripping it. Squirrels, or a weasel maybe, he had thought at first. But by the third trap over a two-mile stretch, he knew something was wrong, and it weren't no weasel.

It was there on his way back, at the third empty trap, that he had seen the track, a paw print larger than his fist. As big, or bigger, than some of the cougar tracks he'd seen, but this was canine, with the tell-tail marks of a dog's non-retractable claws. The traps Lee had set not thirty minutes before, on his way up the narrow little box canyon. He had followed a well-worn game trail and placed his traps near small watering holes fed by the spring at the top. He hadn't trapped this canyon for some time, having left it alone after catching a small cougar some months back.

After setting his final trap, he had hiked up to the mouth of the spring, where the steep walls of the canyon got too narrow to go any further. Stopping by the small pool he brought a scoop of the cold water up to his parched lips and slurped loudly. He drank a few more handfuls and then sat atop a large boulder looking back down the canyon.

His body was tired. He could no longer do the same tasks he used to, at least not with the same amount of ease. He ached more, and it took him longer to get out of bed. This last winter had been tough, keeping enough firewood on hand to heat his little cabin. His semi-arthritic hands still remembered the ache of the cold. He didn't know how many more winters he had in him. The brown stream of tobacco splattered on the ground as he spat and then shoved himself to his feet.

Come on old man, quit belly achin' and get your ass up.

He half trotted back down the trail, wincing at the pain in his knees as he tried to slow himself on the steep slope. He turned his feet sideways to stair-step his way down, and it helped a little. These days he didn't know what was worse, going uphill or going downhill.

He stopped to catch his breath at one of the waterholes where he had set a trap. He knew there wouldn't be anything in it, not yet at least, but he glanced anyway and was surprised to see the bait was gone. He muttered to himself and pulled another piece of bait from his pack. Stepping on the wings of the vicious trap to keep the jaws from severing the few fingers he had left, he placed the bait and reset the trap. He slowly rocked back on his heels lifting his weight from the trap until he was sure the pin held. By the time he reached the third one and saw the track, he didn't bother re-baiting it. He knew it was time to get out of here. He pushed at the sling on his shoulder, dropping his .22 rifle into his aged and callused hands. It was small but it was a weapon nonetheless. And if he laid eyes on this predator, he'd have himself a wolf pelt.

Still, even with the rifle in his hands, he found his feet moving down the canyon trail faster than usual. The sun had long dropped below the edge of the canyon walls and the sky above was beginning to darken. By the time he emerged from the canyon and out onto the flat plains, his neck ached from craning behind him. He breathed a silent sigh of relief; the canyon was beginning to feel a touch claustrophobic.

Hoisting his pack further onto his shoulders, he began the trek back to his cabin. As night set in, Lee's eyes relaxed and his other senses became heightened, mostly his ears, listening for any sign of movement around him. But as he plodded along, all he heard was the occasional skittering of a fright-ened jackrabbit.

He allowed his mind to wander, hoping to pass the time faster. He drifted back to his forties when he had finally married. She had been beautiful. A flower that had managed to wrap herself around the thorn that he was. He had been a rambler and a vagabond all his life, loving the freedom he possessed; but she had been the first that had managed to ground him, the first to make him consider a rooted life. Being a full decade older than she was had put a fair amount of doubt in him, but she didn't care, and so neither did he.

They wed in December at a little church in a little town at the base of the Ruby Mountains. Not exactly the traditional time of year for a wedding, but she loved snow, and her mind was set.

They made a life there in that little town. He trapped and started guiding hunters into the wilderness. The shock came when after three years she got pregnant. He thought he was too old to be having kids and had never pictured himself as a father. But as time wore on he got used to the idea and actually got pretty excited at the prospect.

The morning her water broke had been the scariest morning of his life. He broke every speed limit there was, to get her to the hospital, and he was unbelievably relieved when the nurses pushed her into the delivery room. Seven hours later the doctor was there; Dr. Spade, he remembered, standing before him, telling him how sorry he was and that they had done everything they could do. Something about severe hemorrhaging, and not enough oxygen. But by then Lee was gone, his mind lost in a fog. He still doesn't remember leaving the hospital, just getting out of the truck somewhere up in the mountains. Lee pushed a tear from his eye at the memory; to this day the wound was still as fresh as it ever was.

Lee froze when a crashing sound tore through the brush ahead of him. He stopped and threw up his gun, envisioning a red-eyed timber wolf charging him. Whatever it was, it was large and was moving slowly.

"Owe! Goddammit."

Another crash.

It was a man—the last animal he'd expect to find out here. Lee started to yell out to him but something stopped him. He followed the man for a bit who was splashing a flashlight about, collecting sagebrush. Something didn't seem right and so Lee silently peeled back to go check out the cabin. When he topped the hill he could see three men on the porch bathed in lantern light. He didn't know if they were friendly, but he was definitely outnumbered. He snuck up close enough to hear them and didn't like what he heard. From this distance, he could see one of them was a boy and he was hanging from the rafters. The other men looked rough, like hardened fighters. Lee didn't know what this was about, but he damn sure wasn't going to let some boy get murdered on his porch.

He edged back and dropped his pack. Hefting his rifle he went back to take care of the other one first. It wasn't very difficult to find him; the man was making more noise than an elephant. Lee easily crept up behind him and brought the butt of the rifle down on the base of the man's skull. He crumpled to the ground with a sickening thump. He didn't know if he was dead, but if he wasn't, he'd be eating from a spoon from now on.

Lee hurried back up the hill looking down over the cabin and watched in horror as one man sliced a finger from the boy's hand. The blood-curdling scream that followed sent shivers up Lee's spine. His heart raced, he had to hurry. He was still too far away to make an accurate shot. He tried to creep down the hill as quickly and as quietly as he could but the adrenaline in his veins made him unsteady and his heel found a loose rock. His ankle twisted and he pitched forward, nearly landing on his face. He lifted his head and then froze, listening. The man on the porch was yelling.

"Jack, is that you? Jack?!"

Lee slowly brought his rifle forward, hoping it hadn't been damaged. He propped it up on his arm and put the bead on the man that had been yelling; but as his finger tightened over the trigger, the man ducked inside the cabin. Lee's eyes flicked to the other man who was kneeling next to the boy. He saw a glint of steel as the man slid a knife into the boy's side. He didn't hesitate; he pivoted and squeezed the trigger. Before today, Lee had never killed a man, he had taken the lives of many animals and one thing he knew was the death shot, the movement a body makes when life has been extinguished. It usually happens when a bullet enters the brain or severs the spinal column. The movement is caused by adrenaline or reflexes but lacks the gusto of life.

The man rose from his haunches nearly to a stance and then crumpled sideways falling from the porch. Lee blinked and then noticed the other man leaping into the Humvee. He fired but he knew he missed. The vehicle roared to life and the taillights glowed as it sped off, Lee fired three more times, taking out the front passenger tire. As it turned he fired twice more into the grill, striking the radiator. The Humvee swerved, the bare rims cutting into the road, but it didn't stop. Lee watched as the taillights disappeared over the hilltop.

CHAPTER 5
MISSING PIECES

ANDREW WAS UP AND RUNNING. There was something behind him, chasing him. He was too scared to look back. His fear was stuck in his throat. He felt it getting closer. Someone was yelling at him to run, but he couldn't see them. He kept running but his legs felt like jelly and his feet were heavy, like he was running in sand. The creature was gaining on him. Then he could see her, his mother, yelling for him to run. There was blood running down her face. Suddenly he felt the shift and the thing started running towards her. He tried to scream but he couldn't get out a sound. He tried to run to save her but his feet got even heavier. The thing nearly had her. It was reaching out its claws...

"Mom!"

Andrew jumped up, frantic. He was covered in sweat, tears streaming down his face. He felt the pain in his side as he lurched and it nearly leveled him. The light was blinding and the room was spinning.

"Easy! Take it easy! You're alright. You're safe. Lie back down so you don't tear your stitches. I managed well enough the first time, but it'll be a mess if you tear 'em."

Andrew's heart was racing but he allowed himself to be

eased back into the bed. He was looking at a beard, or a face that was mostly a beard. The gray beard was topped with a shiny, smooth, pink head with a pair of round glasses in between.

"Where am I?" Andrew was able to croak out.

"You're in my cabin on the Mud Meadow Reservoir. You've been out for a few days now. You had a nasty fever but it looks like it finally broke. You're lucky to be breathing kid. Them S.O.B.'s nearly did you in. I patched you up as best I could; I am a bit limited on first aid supplies. But I sewed you up and give ya a shot of penicillin. I think you'd be a goner if I hadn't a popped that fella when I did. I don't think he got that pig sticker in far enough to do you any permanent damage."

The flood of memories came rushing back to him and he jerked his hand up, hoping he had dreamed that part. The heavy wrapping of gauze confirmed that that particular part of the nightmare was real. But hope sparked in him; he could still feel his pinky. He tried to wiggle it but the gauze was too tight. Maybe it hadn't cut completely off or the man reattached it somehow.

"Oh, and that. Almost forgot. I had to cauterize it, couldn't get the damn thing to stop gushing. It ain't easy, losin' a digit. Lost two myself." He said, holding up his hand which was missing both his pinky and his ring finger. "Got 'em caught in a trap a few years back. It hurt like a son of a..."

Andrew cut him off, still confused. "But I can feel it!"

"Yup, that's the way it is with getting something cut off. The nerves make you think it's still there, even makes it feel like you can move 'em."

Andrew's heart sank and he felt sick; he didn't think he'd ever feel whole again. He stared at his big gauze ball of a hand. The old man watched him, knowing too well the hurt and despair Andrew was feeling.

"Are you hungry? I bet you're hungry. I got a whole mess

of stew. Here, let me get you some. I give you what water I could while you were out, but I was scared you'd choke to death if I tried to feed you anything. Then all that work of doctoring you up would've been for nothing."

The man laughed then, a little too heartily.

"You haven't had anyone to talk to for a while have you?" Asked Andrew when the man brought him his stew.

He helped him sit up and Andrew winced when he felt the pull of the stitches.

He laughed again. "Nope, sure haven't. Haven't seen a soul in a couple of months, give or take. Until you lot showed up."

"What happened? How come they didn't know you were here?" asked Andrew before taking a bite of the steaming soup.

He blew on it and then sipped it off the spoon. It was good and his stomach growled as it received the first drops of the warm liquid. Andrew was suddenly aware of his stomach being quite empty. He listened to the man recount his story from the beginning of checking his traps with rapt attention, as he slurped down his stew.

"...now here I am staring at this paw print the size of a horseshoe! So... hey, you're out of stew. Let me get you some more."

"Thank you... uh..."

"Oh by golly. I'm sorry. Lee, Lee Eckart's the name."

"Nice to meet you Lee, I'm Andrew."

"Pleasure, Andrew."

Lee brought him another full bowl of the steaming stew and Andrew slid easily back into the story sipping the hot broth. He marveled at the way the old hermit could tell a story.

"...by the time I got back to the top of the hill, it didn't look good for you, so I got in a bit of a rush coming down the hill and tripped on a rock. They heard me then and I reckon it was me that got you knifed. I could see time was of the essence, so I propped old Delores up on a rock and popped the fella with the knife. The last guy dove into the rig and took off. I popped a couple of his tires but it didn't slow him down none."

"The Commander got away? But they'll come back here!"

"Take it easy, I managed to put one into his radiator too. He didn't make it too far before he had to hoof it. I don't think he'll be in any hurry to come back here anyhow. First, he don't know how many people attacked him, there might have been a lot of us. Second, he was in the cabin, he knows there's not enough supplies in there to bother with, in fact, he took all the canned goods I had left... in the cabin, that is. Don't worry, we're safe for now. You need to get some more rest. Gonna have to let yourself heal up before you try moving around too much."

Andrew was tired, but he felt a sense of urgency and wanted to protest. Once again he felt like a defenseless sitting duck.

"Wait, my pistol! Where's my pistol?"

Lee had gotten up and turned back towards him, pulling a pistol from his belt and looking down at it.

"This it? It was stuck in the belt of the one making all the noise."

"Yeah that's mine; he must have taken it when he clubbed me. My dad gave it to me."

Lee handed it to him butt first and when Andrew took it he turned it over and over, examining it for damage or dirt. Finally satisfied, he slipped it beneath his pillow. Lee chuckled.

"Alright, sonny boy you get some rest."

Andrew sank back into the warmth and comfort of the quilts and the pillow. He slid his hand up until it wrapped around the grip of his pistol and slowly let his eyes close.

CHAPTER 6
LESSONS LEARNED

BEING ON ORDERED BED REST, Andrew spent the next few days recounting his story to Lee. How he had twice escaped the men, only to be bushwhacked when he came to Lee's small lake. When he was done, Lee told Andrew how he had come to be a hermit living off the land in the middle of nowhere.

He had been a buckaroo, or a cow hand, in his younger days. Never being able to stay settled in one place too long, he had worked as a buckaroo all over the western half of the country, moving from one spread to another. He stayed in Montana for the longest stretch, nearly ten years. It was there that he learned to trap. The spring calf crop was being wiped out by cats, and the hired trapper couldn't keep up. He needed help, so Lee volunteered. At that point, all he knew about trapping was what he had seen in movies, which turned out to be mostly wrong anyway.

He quickly fell in love with the occupation. Finding the trails, the watering holes, the beds; setting the traps in such a way as to not be discovered, it all thrilled him to no end. But what he really loved was the wildness of it, the danger, being in the elements. He read every book he could get his hands on, about tracking and trapping.

"That spring we caught twenty-three cats and we still didn't put a dent in them, mind you the ranch we were on was pushing a hundred thousand acres." He said.

Lee spent a lot of time in the wilderness after that, contracting with different ranches to trap, wherever there was a problem with cats, coyotes, or even bears. He started guiding hunters into the wilderness as well. Which he liked for a time, but he quickly grew tired of whiny hunters who wanted him to carry them up to the deer and elk; set them down, let them shoot, and then carry them back out to camp, so they could drink and sit by the fire, while he cleaned and packed out their animal. They certainly weren't all like that, but enough of them were that the occupation soured for him.

Lee started to say something else but stopped himself and Andrew thought he saw the old man wipe a tear from his eye. After a moment, he cleared his throat and continued.

"About that time the government started putting their clinch on the states and calling for the banning of everybody's guns. I had seen enough that I knew what was coming wouldn't be good either way. I sold my house, took my savings, and started buying the supplies and tools I'd need. I even had the spot picked out. Found this place working as a claim-staker some years back. I broke down about ten miles north and stumbled on this little piece looking for cell service. Told myself one day I'd live here, one way or another.

"I was prepared, but still not quite ready to leave society behind, until that damned plague broke out. I packed up and had a friend haul my prefab cabin kit out on a small trailer. It took me almost two months to build this little cabin! Damn instructions were in every language but English!"

"So if you came out here when the outbreak first started then you haven't heard about how bad it got, or the shut-down?" Andrew asked.

"Eh, every spring I haul my pelts into Cedarville and trade for supplies. I don't know the details, but I know how the story played out. How many ended up dying?"

"I don't know. Nobody does, not since the power went out. Millions though. A hundred million in the U.S. was the last official count, I think."

"By God."

Lee looked down at the floor and shook his head slowly, his eyes growing misty. Andrew sat silently, not knowing what to say.

"Decent lookin' bike you got out there. Ought to get you anywhere you want to go."

Andrew looked up, happy for the break in the silence.

"Yeah. My legs aren't quite long enough for it, but I'm starting to manage. Hey, don't you have any kind of transportation?"

"Had a mule but it got lame and died a while back. Figured on picking up a new one this spring. Reckon I'll have to hoof with as many pelts as I can carry when the time comes. Fact is, I got nowhere I'd rather be. Besides I've come to like walking. Keeps me fit and gives me plenty of time to think and enjoy the desert. I do a lotta writing. And when I walk, that's when most of my ideas come to me. Writing is a lot like walking. They are both good for the soul and both help you let go of whatever is eating at you."

Andrew let out a long breath. Thinking about walking only added to the misery of being stuck in bed. His legs itched to walk, to run. Sometimes his skin felt like it was crawling and he wanted to scream. He took another deep breath and willed himself to relax and not think about it.

Andrew sighed and looked out the window. The sun had gone down without him realizing it while listening to Lee's stories. The heat radiating from the potbellied stove and the stars shining out the window made him feel very relaxed and his eyes slowly drifted closed.

"Ready for some dinner?"

Andrew's eyes snapped open and he laughed.

"Sure."

———

"Now step down on the wings, so the mouth opens. Okay, now set the pin. Good. Now slowly let it up to make it sure catches."

Andrew cautiously lifted his feet off the trap.

"Good job kid. I think you got it down. Might make a trapper out of you yet."

Andrew smiled. For the last few days, Lee had been teaching him to track an animal, and now he was learning to set traps. It felt good to be outside and moving around again after being forced to stay in bed for a week. But he was mostly excited about learning from the old trapper. He had always had a passion for learning new things, and this was no exception. His dad had told him once that learning is growing; and if a life-form isn't growing, it's dying. Andrew had been young and it had taken some time for him to figure out what that meant. Eventually, he began to see how there was so much to learn in this world that you could learn anything you want, and if someone stopped learning that meant that they had given up on wanting to grow and just as well be dead.

Andrew was finding it difficult to adjust to having just four fingers on his hand instead of five. He swore he could still feel it move. Often he forgot that it wasn't there, only to feel the heartbreak again. Certain tasks took more caution, although it was healing up quickly. If he pushed it too far or bumped his hand enough it would begin bleeding through his bandages again. Setting the traps was especially difficult at first, but he was determined, and soon he learned to work with his handicap instead of fighting it, and was able to set the traps nearly as quickly as the old trapper.

Over the following days, Lee took him all around the territory that he hunted and trapped, stopping to check and reset each of his traps. They found two traps that had been tripped near where Lee had said he had seen the wolf track. They were extra cautious in the area but never saw a sign of anything. However, Andrew could still feel the hair on the back of his neck standing erect long after they had left the box canyon.

In one of Lee's best spots, they found a coyote that had been caught. They dispatched it and then Lee showed him how to skin it out in such a way that saved all the best fur.

Lee wiped his nose with the back of his hand, so as not to smear his face with his bloody hands.

"When we get back, I'll show you how to clean it and tan the hide."

"Huh? Oh, okay. Cool."

Andrew had been staring at the skinned carcass of the canine. The thin long muscle tissue and gaunt body reminded him too much of a domestic dog, something that was loyal and protective. He understood the need for it, especially now that warm clothing couldn't be bought off the shelf, but decided then that as long as he had warm clothes and wasn't starving, he had no need to kill something he wasn't going to eat; unless of course, they decided to eat him.

When they reached the cabin, Lee started showing him the process of cleaning and tanning the hide. After they had finished, Andrew walked down to the water to wash up. The sun was getting close to the horizon and the water was the color of shimmering gold. The evening was cold but the days had still held their warmth, autumn refusing to give way to winter. Lee walked out of the cabin and joined Andrew at the shore. He was holding a fur hat. It was coyote fur and looked like the ones he had seen in old war movies being worn by Russian soldiers. Lee held it out to Andrew.

"It's called a ushanka. It'll keep you warm even in a blizzard. Try it on."

"You made it?"

Andrew turned it over in his hands, feeling the soft fur.

"Sure did! Had to do something with all my free time out here!" He laughed.

Andrew smiled and knew he was teasing about the free time. It seemed to him that it was a full-time job just to survive out here. He slipped the hat on and it fit perfectly, the warm fur forming to his head.

"It fits!"

"Good. It's yours. In honor of your first kill."

Andrew beamed. He was sure he looked silly, but he didn't care. He wore the hat like a crown.

"It ought to keep you warm on your bike. You'll be able to ride out of here pretty soon I expect. Winters coming on, best not keep your aunt and uncle waiting. If they got word of your parents somehow, they'll be wondering about you."

Andrew winced. He had almost forgotten about getting to his aunt and uncle's. He had allowed himself to dive completely into Lee's way of life and shut out the rest of the world. He liked the old man and the little cabin had begun to feel like home. But Lee was right; he needed to be moving along. It had been nearly three weeks since he had been tortured by the Commander and his men. But he had healed well enough to manage the bike with his hand, and the pain in his side was manageable. Like Lee said, winter was coming, and riding in the snow was not something Andrew thought he'd care to do.

"You're right, I should get going. If it snows, I'll be stuck here until spring. I suppose I should get my things packed up."

"That's fine, but don't plan on leaving 'til the morning. You get a good night's sleep, and then I'll fix ya a hot breakfast before you go."

Lee grinned and headed into the cabin.

Andrew decided to go over his bike and make sure it was ready to travel, having not hardly looked at the thing in weeks. He checked the oil and then looked for leaks, broken hoses, and loose wires. Then he took the air filter out and knocked it against the side of the bike, pouring a small pile of fine powdery dirt onto the ground. He rapped the filter until it stopped dropping dust. That would have to do since he didn't have a way to blow it out. He turned back to the cabin and could hear the old man banging around with pots and pans, preparing the night's meal. Andrew smiled and knew that he'd miss this place and he'd miss the old man. While he had been on bed rest, Lee had read him a lot of his stories. Most of them were about mountain men, cowboys, and shootouts, but there was one Andrew had particularly liked and attempted to commit to memory--

A family of beavers had migrated up a stream and found a valley full of springs that fed the stream. The beavers proceeded to log out the valley and used the timbers to build up an enormous dam. The old grandfather beaver taught the young beavers how to gnaw down the trees so they fell the right way and how to float them downstream so they landed in the right spot to construct the dam properly. Eventually, the springs filled the valley and formed a lake. Trout migrated back up the stream and managed to populate the lake and grew to great numbers. Eagles nested in the valley to take advantage of the abundance of trout. Deer migrated in to feed on all the lush meadows where the trees once stood. Bears came to feed on the deer and the fish.

Then men came and caught the fish, and trapped the beaver, and shot the deer and the bear. Eventually, without the upkeep of the dam by the beavers, it gave way and everything below it was wiped out. The grass, no longer near the water, shriveled and died, and without the protection of the trees, the topsoil washed away, leaving behind the rocks and boulders. Where once there was life, now only a rocky wasteland remained.

Andrew understood the point of the story, or at least thought he had. The beavers came through and destroyed what the valley was. They killed all the trees and flooded the valley, but the result was more abundance than was there before. The area was full of life, but when man came and killed, all he left behind was devastation. Man doesn't operate within the circle of life, the laws of nature. Andrew promised himself to always remember that story.

CHAPTER 7
WHEN ROCKS FLY

AFTER BREAKFAST, Lee had seen him off, but before he did, he gave Andrew his spare rifle, a semi-automatic .22 caliber, which was now strapped to his back along with his duffel bag.

"Not going to take down anything worth eating with that little pistol. Best you have something with a little bit of range." He said.

Andrew hoisted it on his back and strode out to his bike, Lee following. Andrew stopped and turned back casting his eyes down, not knowing what to say. But Lee spoke before he could muster his voice.

"Alright boy, you take care of yourself."

He shook hands with Andrew and then pulled him into a bear hug.

"Now get outta here. You're burning daylight!"

Lee squeezed his shoulder one last time and then turned and walked to the cabin. Andrew pulled down his ushanka and then wiped his eyes. He wanted to thank him, but the words wouldn't come. He watched Lee disappear into the cabin; then he mounted his mud-caked bike and sped off down the road, leaving nothing but a trail of dust that quickly blew away in the wind.

Lee had told him to head southeast until he made it to the salt flats, then turn north and follow the east side of the flats to the Jackson Mountains. Once past those, he should be only one or two valleys over from his aunt and uncle's ranch.

By the time he reached the edge of the salt flats his stomach was growling and he decided to stop for a meal. A large warm rock formed his picnic table, and he marveled at the vastness of the flats while he ate. He heard once that the majority of the Great Basin area was once a massive saltwater lake, and where he was sitting would have been deep underwater. There was evidence of the ancient shorelines on the hillsides, but it was still hard to believe. He tried to imagine the dry arid desert filled up with water, populated by enormous aquatic creatures gliding through the water above his head.

Strange how the world can change so much but we don't get to see it because it takes so long to change.

Andrew finished up his lunch and began packing up, brushing small crumbs of food from his lap. His ears perked up as they caught a noise and his head tilted to listen. He could hear voices. He looked around wildly. Then he heard them again. They were coming from just over the next bluff. He jumped down and pushed his bike behind the rock. He grabbed his rifle and took aim, laying his finger against the trigger just as they crested the hill. His finger tensed. He could see a tall man; he put the barrel on him and then stopped. The man didn't look like part of the 'Restored Republic', but that wasn't what stopped him. With the man was a girl, not much older than Andrew.

Andrew watched them as they walked by, each carrying an arm full of dried branches. He got a better look at the man, he was thin and elderly. They passed within twenty feet of his rock but didn't spot him. He watched as they paced down the next hill. Andrew decided to follow them and see where they were headed. He kept out of sight, hiding behind rocks and keeping to the side hill. As he followed he could just make out their conversation, the old man was talking to the girl.

"...it was a simple case of kill or be killed. Mother Nature was slowly being strangled. Eventually, she had to fight back or she was going to die. Now she's free of the choke hold but the damage has been done. It's going to take a long time to heal, to us anyway. From the perspective of the universe, it will merely be the blink of an eye. Mother Nature will heal herself, that's what she does, but humans are creatures of habit. They are incapable of learning from their past. But that can change, it has to. That's the only way of preventing it from happening again. Mankind mustn't repeat this mistake. That's why it's so important that you understand this, Kaya. It falls to your generation to see that this doesn't happen. You must pass on these lessons in such a way that each generation hereafter knows the importance and continues to pass on the lessons until humans can evolve to a higher level; a point where we wouldn't be capable of this kind of destruction and rape. My generation..."

Andrew cursed under his breath. He had been standing on a pile of rocks to watch them, and the pile had slipped out from underneath his foot echoing the racket through the little draw he was perched in. He heard nothing for a few seconds, then barely caught the old man's hiss.

"Run!"

Andrew panicked. These seemed like safe enough people. He didn't want to scare them off and he definitely didn't want them shooting at him. He had had enough of that. He jumped up.

"Wait! I'm not going to hurt you!"

He saw them turn and look back but they kept on running. So he stood there, trying to decide what to do for a moment. He looked down and realized he was still holding his rifle. He had been waving it over his head to get their attention.

Well, that's one way to look harmless.

Andrew decided to follow them and try to talk to them. He felt bad for having scared them and figured it wouldn't hurt to find out if they had seen anyone else out here recently. There was a good chance the Commander was still alive and if he was, Andrew didn't think he was the kind of man to just let bygones be bygones.

He sauntered over the next little hill and there below in an alcove where the salt flats met the foothills, was an old Winnebago. It was very small and looked like it had seen better days. It was covered in dust and mud and didn't have a window that wasn't cracked. The parts that weren't covered in mud were painted with purple and green symbols. In front of it was a fire pit bordered by a couple of camp chairs and a small table. He could see a line loaded with clothes flapping in the breeze. He started down the hill towards the camp, and out of the corner of his right eye, he saw something flying towards him. Before he could react, it slammed into his upper arm. The pain caused him to drop his gun and grip his arm. He turned to look where it had come from. Another flying object came hurtling towards his head, but this time he dove out of the way just before it crashed into his temple.

Rocks! They're throwing freaking rocks at me!

Andrew rolled and came up but as he did so a large one caught him in the stomach, knocking the wind out of him. He ran, hunched over, gasping for breath. He scooped up his gun and ran straight away from the origin of the flying rocks. When he was sure he was out of range, he stopped and turned. They continued throwing but the fist-sized rocks were landing five to ten feet short of where he was standing. He cupped his hand to the side of his mouth.

"I have a gun! Don't you think I would have used it by now if I wanted to hurt you?!"

"Not if you don't have any bullets! You were probably going to use the empty gun to try to rob us!" shouted the old man.

Andrew couldn't believe it. He stood there dumbfounded. He glanced down at the camp to his left. On the table, he could see a tin can. He took aim with his rifle and fired. The empty can flipped up through the air. He glanced over at the two, who were watching the flying can in silence. The can landed a few feet from the fire pit. He sent it flying through the air once more, to show that not only did he have bullets, but that he had enough that he didn't mind wasting a couple, even though he did mind. He rested the gun in the crook of his crossed arms, in a relaxed posture. He watched them. They were talking back and forth. Finally, the old man turned back to him.

"What do you want?" he shouted.

"Just to talk. I'm making my way across the desert, trying to get to my aunt and uncle's. I lived west of here, just into California. We were attacked and... my parents were killed. All I wanted to know was if you had seen anyone else in the area, and if I knew it was going to be this much trouble, I would have gone right on by!"

"Why were you sneaking up on us?"

"I was hiding. I wanted to be sure you weren't part of the group that attacked me. They have been chasing me for a ways. I wanted to be cautious."

They were silent for a few minutes talking amongst themselves. Then finally the old man stepped out from the cover of their rock, holding up his hands.

"Alright, we are coming out."

Andrew slung the rifle over his shoulder, hoping that would put them at ease. His pistol was still on his belt and he knew if they tried anything he was a lot faster with it anyway, but at least he looked less intimidating.

He studied the old man. He was an odd-looking character,

wearing a small rounded felt hat. The kind you see in movies from the twenties and thirties, a bolo hat, he thought they were called. From under the hat trailed two long gray braids resting on each of the man's shoulders. The ends were tied with leather.

Andrew was marveling at the old man's tie-dyed clothes when he realized he probably looked equally strange. Between his fur ushanka, his bloodied and torn jacket, and his assortment of guns, he must look like quite the vagabond.

His mind, however, lost all train of thought when the girl appeared from behind the rock. Despite the grime and disheveled hair something about her made his heart race and his head light. Her hair was dark brown, lightly bleached in spots by the sun. It was pulled back into a single braid. She was wearing a filthy and tattered Trader Joe's sweatshirt and a set of worn-out jeans, whose condition Andrew couldn't tell if it was just from wear, or if they had been bought that way.

Their eyes met and he smiled a bit but she cast her gaze down to the ground. Tearing his eyes away from her, he strode up to the old man with his hand out in a sign of friendship and they shook.

"I'm Andrew."

"I am Jupiter and this is Kaya, my granddaughter."

"Hello," she greeted him quietly.

"Hi," said Andrew.

"Let's go down to camp. We can sit and talk. We have some quinoa we can share."

Andrew wasn't exactly sure what keen-wah was, but he was glad to be on friendlier terms with these people. The girl set about lighting a campfire and Jupiter motioned for Andrew to take the camp chair across from him. He leaned the rifle against the chair and took his seat. Once the fire was lit, the girl put on a pot of water to boil. She stayed kneeling there next to her grandfather, not looking up, just staring into the flames.

"So you say your parents were killed? I am sorry to hear that. Kaya's parents are also dead. They were killed by the virus, just like so many others. If you don't mind my asking, who was it that attacked you?"

Andrew took a deep breath and retold the story once again. This time he avoided the details of how he found his parents; then went on to tell them about being tortured by the Commander and his men, brandishing his stub of a pinky, and then continued with Lee's timely rescue. Jupiter listened attentively, obviously fascinated by the story. Even Kaya tore her gaze from the fire and stared at Andrew, eyes wide, as he described his trials. When he was done, Jupiter sat back in his chair and looked like he was pondering deeply as he twisted his pointed beard between his thumb and finger.

"How much further do you have to go to get to your uncle's ranch?"

"I'm not sure exactly. But it shouldn't be more than two or three days on my bike."

Andrew figured these people were harmless enough, but his experience had taught him to be cautious, and in desperate times people did desperate things. The exact location of his aunt and uncle's ranch wasn't something he was about to reveal to anyone. He decided he should try to steer the conversation away, so there wouldn't be any more questions.

He studied their faces. Their eyes looked sunken and dark, and their cheekbones drew heavy shadows upon their faces. He hadn't noticed before, but they both looked to be starving.

"Can I ask you a question? What are you doing out here?"

"Surviving. The Bay Area just kept getting worse. Riots, murders, looting, and the north coast wasn't much better. I had to get her to safety. We left three months ago. We were headed for the playa, but it was deserted so we kept going north, knowing there was another town just over the border.

However, a heavy rainstorm came through and well you can see the results. We are stuck here."

Andrew glanced back at the tires of the RV buried deep in the mud.

"The ground seems drier now. Have you tried again?"

Jupiter shook his head.

"Unfortunately we ran out of fuel a few days ago. I ran the engine intermittently to keep the batteries charged and the icebox cold to keep the few perishables we had from spoiling."

Steam rose from the pot and the water slowly began to boil. Kaya poured in the contents of a small plastic bag and began stirring with a wooden spoon.

"That's the last of it," she said without looking up.

Jupiter looked down at the pot and then at her. He stared at his granddaughter for a long time and Andrew saw tears brimming in the man's eyes. Finally, he looked up at Andrew.

"Walk with me, Andrew?"

He stood and waited. Andrew got up, threw the rifle back over his shoulder, and matched pace with the old man as he headed towards the hills. Jupiter was silent until they had crested the first small hill and were out of earshot of the camp. He swallowed hard before he started, staring out at the horizon.

"Andrew, we're starving. We shouldn't have come out here. I used to come every year for the festival and thought how rugged and wild this country is. Figured this would be the place to escape the chaos of humanity and live off of the land. I thought that others would come too and we could build a community together. Someone did come to the playa; there was a car and a few tents. But it was deserted, probably all dead. I've tried to forage and even to hunt, but I know nothing about living in the wild. I was a fool. Now my stupidity may have killed me and my granddaughter. I can't bear to watch that happen. She's all I have left, Andrew. I beg you, take her with you. It's the only way she stands any chance of surviving."

Andrew's heart caught in his throat.

"I... I can't. I have food. You can have it, most of it... and I can teach you how to hunt. Maybe we can find gas and figure out how to get you out of here."

He was in no way prepared to take on the responsibility of keeping this girl safe. He could barely keep himself safe. Besides, he had enough trouble handling the bike when it was just him. He had carried passengers before but that was on his nimble little dirt bike, not this five-hundred-pound behemoth.

Jupiter was silent for a while. Finally, he nodded and cast his eyes to the ground.

"Alright. Thank you, Andrew."

CHAPTER 8
SHARED APPLES

THE NEXT DAY Andrew did his best to give a crash course to them on what he had learned about hunting and trapping from Lee. He showed him how to set up a small snare, how to find game trails, what few plants could be eaten, and how to properly identify them. The latter seemed to be the only part Kaya was interested in. At a small spring about a mile from the RV, where Jupiter and Kaya had been getting water, Andrew speared a handful of small frogs. That night, he and Jupiter dined on fried frog and baked beans, but when Andrew offered one of the hopping morsels to Kaya she refused.

"Don't tell me you're not hungry."

Kaya, lips tight, shook her head.

"She's vegetarian, Andrew. At least have some beans, Kaya. I checked, there's no meat in them."

"Uhh... oh... sorry. I didn't know. Here..."

Andrew quickly scooped out a portion of the steaming beans for her.

"Thanks," said Kaya quietly, carefully taking the beans.

Silence rose from the campfire while everyone ate, but Andrew's mind was ablaze with disbelief.

A vegetarian? How the hell have they survived this long out here?

After he ate, he settled into his sleeping bag, his head resting on his jacket, rolled up against the wheel of his motor-cycle. With his head propped up, he gazed out over the fading horizon and the multiplying shimmers of the stars. He took a deep breath of night air, willing himself to relax. He spotted a flashing light moving across the sky. His heart leaped, thinking for a moment that it was an airplane; but the realization hit that it was merely an orbiting satellite, sending signals that no one could hear.

———

Two days after he arrived, Andrew decided to take his bike out and do some scouting. Across the salt flats, the mountains rose much higher and Andrew hoped there would be more game and maybe more vegetation, but late fall yielded little in the high desert. Still, he had to try. His other goal was to get high enough to see if there were any settlements where he might be able to find gas for their RV.

A low growl caused Andrew to rub his stomach as he dug through the food stuffed in his pack. Supplies were getting low and he'd have to skip breakfast. He pulled out an apple and a can of string beans for later. There seemed to be a lot of string beans. The watery, bitter-tasting beans had once been something he had refused to eat. His mom had given up trying to get him to like them after a few years of arguing at the dinner table. He laughed, staring at the can.

I could be starving to death, and they'd still suck.

"What's so funny?" said Kaya as he shoved the can into the pocket of his coat.

"Huh? Oh, nothing. Just... good morning."

He flashed a smile, trying to cover up his embarrassment.

"Good morning," she said yawning.

Kaya stretched out her arms and bent her back, then folded forward pressing her palms to the ground. Andrew caught his eyes drifting down her lean body and muscular legs that were covered in tight stretchy black leggings. He quickly busied himself with closing up his pack and leaned it back against the RV.

"Going somewhere?"

"Yeah, I'm gonna go do some scouting. See if I can find some food or maybe a place with gas."

"Oh, can I come?"

"I uh... well I... not very good on this bike to take a passenger."

Did that even make sense?

"It's okay. I've ridden on the back of a motorcycle before. I know what to do. I'll go get my sweatshirt."

Shit.

"But what about Jupiter?"

"He's still asleep, he'll be fine."

She disappeared into the RV and was back out in a flash before Andrew was able to think up another objection.

"I'm ready."

Andrew, out of excuses, pulled out another apple from the bag and stuffed it into his pocket.

"Well, uh, okay let's go then."

He mounted his bike and planted his feet firmly on the ground to hold it steady.

"You can..."

Before he could finish she had thrown her leg over, mounted the bike, and wrapped her arms around him. The blood drained from his head as her arms squeezed him tight. His legs wobbled a bit and he had to catch himself from falling over. He drew in a deep breath and punched the ignition button, stirring the single-cylinder engine to life. His thoughts drifted to how warm her legs felt against the outside of his thighs as he eased out the clutch and the bike lurched forward, killing the engine.

"Shit," he hissed through gritted teeth.

"Must still be cold."

His face suddenly felt very hot. He didn't wait for a response, pushing the ignition again as fast as he could. When the engine fired he let it idle a moment and then slowly twisted the throttle as he eased out the clutch, determined to not kill it again.

The undisturbed crust of the salt flats made for a smooth ride, something Andrew wasn't used to. He kept having the sensation that the bike was sliding out from under him, but every time he glanced down everything was fine. He did his best not to think about the tight, black, nylon-clad legs and the warm arms wrapped around him; he was having enough trouble driving as it was. It wasn't terribly different riding with a passenger, but the added weight meant leans and turns had to be done more deliberately. But by the time they reached the far foothills, he was feeling comfortable once again, with the bike at least.

The trail was a rocky one, mostly just a jackrabbit trail, but it wasn't very steep and it took them to the top of the first of the foothills. From there the sagebrush was thicker and the hill got gradually steeper. Andrew squeezed the clutch and they rolled to a stop.

"I think we'll walk from here."

"Okay."

Kaya was off as soon as he had switched off the motor. Andrew pulled himself off to find Kaya standing there staring at him.

"So, where to?" She said, nearly rocking on her heels.

"Umm, up I guess. Let's try to find a good lookout and see if we spot anything."

"Sweet."

Kaya led the way up the hill, no trail, just straight up. Within minutes, Andrews's thighs were burning and his lungs heaving. The scar at the base of his ribs ached like a muscle being stretched too far.

"Kaya... let's take a break."

When she stopped and looked back her face was flush and she was breathing as hard as he was.

"Sure... if you need to stop."

That jab hurt worse than his scar, but he pushed it aside, he had to rest. The cold air made his throat and lungs burn. He did his best to slow his breathing and inhale through his nose.

After a few moments he caught his breath and they pressed on.

"Andrew?"

"Hmm?"

He was concentrating on not slipping on the slick dry grass blanketing the hillside.

"How old are you?"

He had to think for a moment.

"Uh... sixteen. My birthday was this past summer."

"Wouldn't it be every summer?"

"Well... I... yeah."

Andrew sighed, and Kaya laughed.

"Sorry, just teasing!"

"What about you?"

"Seventeen. Not that it matters anymore, age. No driver's licenses, no bars to get ID'ed; things like that seem to lose importance once they don't exist anymore!"

"Right."

Andrew laughed a bit but was only half-listening. He was still stuck on the fact that she was older than him. He didn't know why it bothered him, but it did.

"So were there many things to do where you're from? I

mean, what'd you do for fun out in the middle of nowhere?" she asked.

"There's lots of things to do!"

His voice sounded more defensive than he had intended, so he quickly continued.

"Hunting, fishing, hiking, swimming..."

"Could do without the hunting. Besides, that all sounds like work. Except swimming. I like to swim. I love swimming at the beach."

"It's not work, or at least it didn't used to be. It was fun. I used to hunt and fish with my friends... and my dad."

Andrew choked back the memory and tried to continue.

"I used to ride dirt bikes a lot too. You could ride horses, go arrowhead hunting, hang out with friends, have a bonfire..."

"Ooh, a bonfire! That *would* be fun! We could never do something like that in the city!"

"See there are some perks to being a backwoods redneck."

He said it without much enthusiasm, still feeling a little on the defensive side.

"I didn't call you backwoods!"

"But still a redneck?" he asked, raising an eyebrow.

She turned and smiled then. He was okay with that. Andrew smiled too. Her smile was rather infectious.

"So what about you? What did you do for fun?"

Kaya stopped and sighed.

"Go shopping, explore the city, go to parties, cruise the bay on my friend's parents' sailboat." Said Kaya, sighing.

"That sounds nice. Do you know how to sail? That's something I always wanted to do."

Andrew was beginning to enjoy the conversation.

"Mmm, I know the basics. As long as the weather was good and it was a small enough boat I could probably handle it."

They were both silent for a bit, each picturing white-crested waves and clear blue skies. Andrew was the first to break the silence.

"I haven't seen the ocean since I was eight."

"Really?! Oh my god! It's been less than a year for me and I miss it like crazy. I love the ocean. The sound of the waves, the smell in the air, the fog..."

"You miss the fog?"

"Well, yeah, I love the fog. On a cold day, my friends and I would go down to the wharf and eat lunch at the deli-catessen. We'd settle into a nice warm booth and try to spot boats and seals moving through the mist."

"That does sound nice."

"It was. If we make it out of here alive, I have to go back someday."

"I'd like to go back too."

"Well, maybe we could go together. I could show you some really cool spots. I bet you'd like Muir Woods. The redwoods are amazing. Such ancient creatures, you can almost feel their souls."

"I'd like that."

They both smiled. They crested a knoll then and looking around Andrew suddenly realized how long they'd been climbing.

"This is probably high enough to get a good view."

He was scanning the horizon and his eyes almost immedi-ately shifted to the south to a dense patch of green.

"Are those trees? That looks like a town!"

"Oh yeah, we came through that on the way here. It's tiny, not even a real grocery store, just a little convenience store slash gas station and a handful of houses."

"What? Why didn't you guys tell me? I could have been looking for gas this whole time!"

"We... well, it was deserted. We didn't think there would

be anything there and we were so close to the playa, Jupiter didn't think we'd need anything else."

"... and look how that turned out!"

"Hey! Don't yell at me. I didn't ask to come here! He brought me out here. I never wanted to leave my home in the first place!"

She was near tears and Andrew knew he had pushed too far. He exhaled, calming himself.

"Here, never mind about that. It doesn't matter I can go look for gas once we get back. Do you want a snack?"

He pulled an apple from his pocket and handed it to her and was about to hand her one of the cans, but she briskly turned and started down the hill.

"Aren't you going to eat?"

"I'll eat *mine* at the bottom!"

Something about her tone told Andrew that he had best eat his at the top.

———

They made the drive back in silence. Kaya refused to speak when he had come down the hill and Andrew, at a loss for what to say, joined her. When they reached the camp, Jupiter was running around waving his arms excitedly at them. Andrew pulled up to a stop and let down his kickstand, waiting for Kaya to dismount.

"We got one! We got one! I was trying to figure out what to do, but then I saw your dust then figured I would just wait!"

"Got what?" asked Andrew.

"A rabbit! We got a rabbit!"

Andrew heard Kaya gasp, but she said nothing. Andrew climbed off the bike and Jupiter led them to the snare. He could hear the struggling animal before he saw it. The snare was a kind that merely lassoed the animal's foot, not killing it.

Andrew walked up and pulled his knife from his pocket, ready to cut off its head, when a shrill scream sent shivers up his spine. Rabbits were known to make quite a racket when they had been wounded or attacked. However, this shriek had come from Kaya, not the rabbit. Andrew spun to look at her and as he did so, she ran forward, tore the snare free, and released the rabbit. In two great hops, he disappeared into the sagebrush.

"What the hell are you doing?" Andrew shouted at her.

"Keeping you from killing a defenseless animal!" she screamed back.

"What? That was our dinner! What do think we are doing out here? I'm teaching you how to stay alive! Where do you think food comes from?"

"The ground! I am a vegetarian and there's plenty of canned food left, and we can find more wild vegetables out here. You just don't know how to find them!"

"First of all, that was my food that I chose to share with you, but it has disappeared twice as fast as I thought it would. Second of all, you don't get the luxury of being a vegetarian out here. Vegetables don't just magically grow here. This is the desert and it's nearly winter. If you want to live you're going to have to eat what's here."

Andrew didn't mean to explode but the town issue and now this drove him to the brink.

"I will not take a creature's life just so I can eat. It's inhumane and cruel!"

Jupiter started to say something to Kaya to calm her down, but Andrew cut him off.

"You know what happens when you don't eat? You die! This isn't San Francisco, it's the wilderness and it will kill you. There's no organic supermarket for you to go and buy your kale and apples! If you ever do that again I will leave you here to starve on your own and good luck finding carrots and celery out here!"

Kaya's eyes flashed and then they started to fill with tears.

She covered her face with her hands and ran back to the RV. Andrew blew out a deep breath of frustration and after a few tense moments, Jupiter spoke.

"I'm sorry. She's a good soul, never been one to harm animals. Neither was I, but I know out here it is necessary for our survival. I'll go and have a talk with her, and make sure it doesn't happen again."

"It's okay, I can talk to her. I shouldn't have snapped. This can't be easy for her, because I know it's not for me."

He blew out another long breath.

"I spotted the town to the south. Why didn't you tell me about it? I could have been searching for gas or food there."

"Oh. Well... when we came through I didn't feel the need to stop because we were so close, but once we got stuck here, it was too far to walk with my bad knee and I couldn't send Kaya alone. When you showed up I was too distracted... I suppose my mind hasn't been working all that well."

"I see. Well, I'm going to check it out. With a little luck, I might be able to find some gas."

"We are forever in your debt Andrew. You're a good soul, too. Providence moves for a reason."

Andrew just smiled, not knowing how to respond.

"I guess I'll go speak to Kaya, then I'll get going."

He found Kaya inside the RV. She was sitting with her feet on the couch, her knees up, her arms wrapped around them, with her head down and her body shaking.

"Kaya, is it alright if I come in?" he said, standing on the wobbly iron step.

No response, except a sob as her body continued another bout of shaking. Andrew stepped inside and knelt in front of her. She looked so sad and vulnerable; he wanted to comfort her somehow. But being this close to her made him nervous. He wasn't sure why. He built up the courage to put his hands on her feet, in a feeble attempt to comfort her. The room seemed loud, and he felt his heartbeat in his temples.

"Kaya, I'm sorry for yelling at you. I know this can't be easy for you. It's difficult for me and I even grew up out here. Everything's gonna be alright. We'll find food. I'm going to go check out that town and see if I can find any gas. If I find enough, we may be able to get you guys out of here. Back somewhere safe. Kaya? Stop crying, please? Look at me."

She slowly looked up at him through red swollen eyes and he smiled. He had never seen a prettier face in his life. A hint of a smile broke through the crease of her lips.

"Really? You think we could get out of here?" she said sniffling.

"As long as I can find enough gas... yes, I think maybe we can get you out of here."

This time a full-fledged smile spread across her lips.

"You're going now?"

"Yes, I want to make sure I don't run out of daylight."

"Then you'll need this for luck."

She scooted forward and put her feet down on the floor. She wrapped his face in her hands and slowly leaned forward and kissed him. It was just a peck, and then she was up and out the door before he had even registered what had happened. Quick as it was, its effects loitered in his head and every inch of his skin felt electrified. He stood and his legs felt wobbly. His heart pounded in his chest.

He stepped outside and there she was sitting across from him tending to the fire as though nothing had happened. She didn't even look up at him, but Andrew thought he could see a hint of a smirk on her face. Jupiter came back and dropped a load of twisted branches of dry sagebrush next to her.

"Well... I... I suppose I should get going. I'll be back before dark, I hope."

"Good luck Andrew! Thank you again for going. Fortune be with you!" Said Jupiter.

Andrew threw the sling of his rifle across his shoulder and mounted his bike. He noticed that he was already getting better at managing the bike, or else he was getting taller. He looked at his gear bag still leaning against the RV and decided to leave it. He'd need room for a gas can if he found one. His head was still spinning from the kiss but he managed to get the bike rolling without dropping it on its side in front of his two audience members, although, only one mattered.

CHAPTER 9
CRY WOLF

GIRLS ARE WEIRD.

Andrew was sure she had started to hate him after the day's events. But now, well, he didn't know what to think. He drove past the Burning Man Festival site, known as Black Rock City. Just as Jupiter had said, there was one car and a few tattered tents. Andrew stopped to check the car for gas just to make sure. He tied a small hex nut that he found in the open trunk to a string and dropped it down the throat of the tank. He heard it clatter to the bottom. It sounded dry. He pulled it out and found just part of the nut to be wet. It would take too long and be too much effort for what little bit might be left. He decided to press on.

Kaya entered his mind again; the way her cheek dimpled when she smiled, the way her pants fit tight over her lean hips. Andrew didn't even notice the dust-coated pavement until he was on it. He let out a sigh of pleasure. The smooth pavement felt like sitting down in a soft recliner after spending eight hours in a metal stadium chair. He leaned left and he leaned right, weaving back and forth, getting a feel for the road. He let off the throttle a bit, shifted into his last gear, and then gunned it. The air felt good blowing in his face.

As he rounded the corner, the little town came into view. The sight of it sent a shiver up Andrew's back for some reason. He couldn't figure out what bothered him about it, but something made him uneasy. He slowed down, coasting below twenty-five, unconsciously eying the speed limit sign.

The houses were abandoned. Through broken windows, dirty curtains were beckoned out into the breeze. The bare trees and the leaf-strewn streets gave the tiny town a desolate, haunted look. Andrew decided not to spend any more time here than he had to. He wished he could have brought Kaya or even Jupiter. Another person there with him would have put him a lot more at ease. It was too quiet.

Andrew stopped at the first house that had a car in the driveway. He got off his bike, leaned his rifle against it, and loosened his pistol in its holster. He took his string and nut out of his pocket to check the tank. It was a newer-style car with a little metal flapper at the mouth of the tank. The nut squeezed past his fingers holding the small flap. Finally, gravity took over and he felt the nut tug at the string as it fell. A dry clang at the bottom echoed in the tank. His heart sank. He worked the nut out and wasn't surprised to see it completely dry. He looked around; desperately hoping this wouldn't be the case with all the cars in town.

The hairs on the back of Andrew's neck stood on end. He had the odd feeling he was being watched. He was scanning the houses on the opposite side of the street when his eyes settled on something in the window of the house directly across from him. He stared at the shape inside the shadowy house. Something about it looked out of place but he couldn't put his finger on what it was. Then, in a flash, it was gone. His heart stopped beating and every muscle in his body froze. He couldn't expand his lungs and take a breath. There was someone in the house and they had been watching him. Every horror movie he had ever seen replayed in his mind.

After a moment he was able to calm himself, his breath

coming in large gulps. His feet were still frozen to the cracked sidewalk where he stood. He couldn't decide what to do. He wanted to leave, to run.

There was someone in the house, but maybe they didn't want to be bothered. Maybe they'd shoot him, thinking he was coming after their food. Then again, maybe they were alone, starving, needing help. Maybe they knew where there was gas.

A memory flashed in his mind of his father talking to him. It had been the day his parents had bought him his motorcycle. He had wanted it so bad, but in the first five minutes of riding, he had fallen and sprained his wrist. It had scared him; he had thought it would be like riding a bike. But, it wasn't. Ashamed, he told his parents, eyes blurred with tears, that he couldn't ride it. He was too scared to get on it again. That's when his father told him that they could take the bike back if he wanted them to, but in life, things can be difficult and scary.

'Most often the best thing to do is the scariest thing to do. It's what makes us stronger, turns us into the people we want to be. We grow by doing the difficult things, that scare us, that are out of our comfort zone. Life will fight you every step of the way when you are on the right path because life wants to know if you have got what it takes before it gives you what you want.'

Andrew had left the bike sitting for two weeks, doing his best to ignore it. But every time he looked at it he felt a pang of fear in the pit of his stomach. Finally, sick of seeing it parked in the backyard collecting dust, he mustered up the courage. With shaking hands, he got on it and he rode it. He fell almost immediately but got back up. He fell again and again, but each time he got back up, and soon he wasn't falling anymore.

Now as he stared at the house, he felt that same pang of fear, and then his dad's words echoed in his ears. He wouldn't let fear stop him from finding fuel and getting his friends to safety. He took a deep breath and walked towards the house. He watched the window for more movement but saw none. As he walked up the sidewalk, he noticed the front door was open.

Why would the door be open?

He listened but heard nothing. He took a step through the door and waited. Nothing.

"Hello? My name is Andrew, I'm not looking for trouble. I'm just trying to find a little gas. Hello?"

Nothing.

The hairs on the back of his neck felt like needles. He pulled the pistol from his belt and slid the safety off. This person might be friendly, but then again they might not. He walked across the living room to the first door. It was open just a crack; he pushed on it with the barrel of his pistol. He stepped in and scanned the room. Nothing. The closet was open and empty. He walked to the next bedroom and checked it. Still nothing. He called out again. This time his voice betrayed his fear, it cracked and was barely audible. He cleared his throat and called again. No response.

Then, he heard something, the sound of a can falling to the ground. He gripped his gun tight and walked back across the living room to the kitchen. He heard a noise again but wasn't sure what it was. He thought he heard a humming in his ears, but it was rough. He popped his jaw to clear his ear canal, but he still heard it. He slowly walked around the counter; there were food scraps and feces all over the floor, and the room stunk. The sound grew louder, it was gravelly and deep. He stepped to the door of the pantry. There, standing over a chunk of maggot-ridden meat, with teeth bared, was a wolf.

With every vein and every airway frozen, Andrew took a step back; and as if that was the signal it was waiting for, the wolf lunged. In one fluid motion, Andrew raised his arm and fired. Either he missed or the bullet had no effect on the massive creature because it kept coming. Andrew fired again, backpedaling. This time he heard a squeal. His heel caught something on the ground and he fell back. His arm swung out grasping the air, and his fingers caught the edge of a cabinet, jerking him to the side. He saw a flash of gray over him, and then it was gone.

Andrew scrambled up, his feet kicking at the torn linoleum. He ran to the door and caught a glimpse of gray fur floating over a short chain-link fence, then disappearing into the desert.

He was shaking uncontrollably. Slamming the door shut, he slid to the floor against it. He needed to get out of there before it came back. Air filled his lungs and he forced himself up. Standing on wobbly knees, he spotted a small blood trail leading out the door. So, he had hit it. It was a fair amount of blood, but it was a big animal, he doubted the wound would kill it. There was still a good chance it would come back, but he still needed to find gas.

He looked out the front door. There were no other cars that he could see on the street. He decided to check the back-yard; the owners should have had a lawn mower and lawn mowers run on gas. If he could find a couple, he might be able to collect enough gas. Scanning the dry, yellow, grass-covered yard through the sliding glass doors, there was no lawn mower out, but he spotted a utility shed in the corner of the yard.

Got to be in there.

He looked around before stepping out, keeping his pistol at the ready. It was a small shed, with a barn-style door. Its roof was missing a few shingles, and the thick white paint on it was peeling. The latch had a padlock on it, but when he looked at it he saw it was unlocked. The padlock landed in the yellow grass as he tossed it aside and pulled open the latch; all the while checking behind his back to make sure his furry friend wasn't sneaking up behind him.

He swung open the large door and peered inside, his eyes

taking a moment to adjust to the darkness. Sure enough, there in the shadows, playing anchor to the suspension bridge of cobwebs was a dusty old lawn mower. He batted at the webs and pulled the mower back towards the light of the door. He removed the gas cap and dropped his string and nut down, and he heard a small plunk, like a penny tossed into a fountain. He let it sink to the bottom and then pulled it out, examining the string. The string was wet a good four inches above the nut. It wasn't enough to go on, but it was a good start. He suddenly realized he had no way of packing it. He needed a container to haul the gas on his bike. He looked around at the dusty, forgotten contents of the shed. Shelves ran the length of each side, filled with rusty tools and a few boxes marked-- Christmas Lights. Then he spotted what he was looking for. There in the corner sat a red, plastic, fuel tank.

Perfect. If I can find a little more gas, I can fill this tank and tie it right to the back of my bike.

He bent over to snatch it up and was surprised at its weight. It was full. He took it out into the light and took off the cap just to make sure of its contents. Sure enough, as he peered inside, the unmistakable smell of gas vapors wafted up and stung his nose. He secured the cap tightly and headed back for his bike. This would be more than enough to get the RV back to the main highway. Besides he didn't think he'd be able to carry much more than that on his bike. He felt a pain in his heart as the realization hit that Kaya would be leaving and he probably wouldn't ever see her again.

Maybe I can convince them to come with me to the ranch.

The idea gave him hope and made him feel warm. He cautiously made his way back through the house and out into the street, scanning for the wolf. But he saw no sign of it. Strapping the jug to the rack on the tail of his bike, he gave one more look around before slinging his rifle back on his shoulder and climbing on. He squeezed the clutch and punched the starter. Using his feet he backed it down onto the street, straightened out, and then rode away. He couldn't get up to speed fast enough. He would be glad to leave the ghost town and the wolf behind.

It was the first time in his life he had seen a wolf. It had nearly killed him. Had he not shot it and fell to the floor at just that moment, he was sure he'd be dead. It had been terrifying, a feeling that Andrew was growing all too familiar with. This single wolf easily could have torn out his throat and gone about his day. He couldn't imagine having to face more than one of the beasts. Andrew shuddered at the thought. He hoped very much that he'd never see one again.

Andrew followed the pavement out of town for about ten miles until he came to the fork in the road where his dirt road met the highway. He already missed the smoothness of the pavement as he veered right and settled into the slower pace demanded by the gravel.

He was only a couple of miles away and could already see the smoke from the campfire. He glanced to the west. It would be getting dark soon. He glanced back towards the camp. There was something wrong. The smoke, there was too much of it, it was black and coming from something much bigger than a campfire.

He sped around the next bend and could see a massive orange glow. The RV was on fire. He could see the long shadows of men cast from the glow of the fire and the sinking sun. The silhouette of one caught his eye. The man's presence was unmistakable; the Commander. He had found him.

Please, God, let Kaya be alive.

CHAPTER 10
JUPITER'S TALK

KAYA HAD DECIDED to go for a walk after Andrew had left. Her hands were trembling and she didn't know why or how to make them stop. No, that wasn't true. She knew why. But why had she kissed him? She needed to get out, away from the camp and away from Jupiter. She needed to think.

When he came to apologize, he had put his hands on her bare feet. It had scared her a little, but his hands had been warm and they sent a feeling of comfort throughout her body. She had wanted those hands wrapped around her then, to hold her. She had felt like a silly little girl throwing a temper tantrum and was embarrassed.

She hadn't really wanted to see him, especially with her sobbing like a baby, but she wasn't in any mood to stop him. She hadn't even heard much of what he was saying; she was thinking about how good his hands felt. But when he had said that he was leaving, it jerked her out of her stupor. When he said he would try to find gas to help get them out, she remembered all he had done for them, and she had felt the irresistible urge to kiss him. Before she knew it, she had his face in her hands and she had kissed his lips. The shock of what she had just done hit her in the chest like a punch. She had to get out before he saw how red her cheeks must have been. She had nearly tripped in her hurry to escape the rising heat inside the Winnebago. She couldn't even bring herself to look at him when he was getting ready to leave.

Kaya picked up a small rock and threw it down the trail she was aimlessly following. The idea of leaving excited her and she couldn't wait to get back to some sort of civilization, but felt an ache when she thought of leaving Andrew. Aside from what had happened in the RV, she had simply gotten used to him being around. Her grandfather wasn't usually much for company. She got tired very quickly of his ranting and raving about all the conspiracies and how this all could have been prevented. She welcomed the company of anyone else to break up the monotony.

She didn't have the typical granddaughter relationship with Jupiter. She barely had any relationship with him at all. The last time she had seen him, she had been six or seven. Her parents didn't exactly get along with him and his eccentric ways. Her dad and Jupiter had had a falling out when she was little. She had lived with her parents in their flat in downtown San Francisco. Both her parents worked long-hour office jobs, but they took care of her and gave her everything she could want. Her parents had balked when she told them she wanted to be a vegan at the age of nine. Over time they accepted it and supported her but she remembered her dad saying that she would turn out to be a hippie just like her grandpa.

She loved playing on the wharf with her friends, visiting all the little shops, and watching the street performers. Riding the ferries from the pier to Sausalito was something she especially enjoyed; the feel of the salty spray while the wind blew in her face, turning her hair into a dancing sea creature. Watching the islands float by with their glamorous villas perched on the steep hillsides.

It was on the ferry that she had first seen someone infected with the virus. At the time everyone thought it was still confined to cows and stuff. She vividly remembered the crimson blood on the handkerchief the man was coughing into on the ferry. The President's announcement had aired that same night.

Her parents were both dead within a week. The city was in chaos, the hospitals were filled to the point of spilling over and the police were doing all they could to control the riots and the panic. She didn't know who else to call and found Jupiter's number in her dad's Rolodex. Jupiter had shown up that same day in his psychedelic RV, wearing a gas mask. She was sure she had made a huge mistake when she saw him, but she knew she didn't have much of a choice.

He had taken her to his cabin further up the coast. They lived there for a while, getting by on what little food Jupiter grew in his small greenhouse. It was mostly occupied by things you could smoke, not eat. But they made do.

One night Jupiter's garden was raided, but he was shocked to see all they took were the vegetables. A few days later, in the evening, Jupiter and Kaya had gone for a walk out on the beach. When they returned, they found the door of the cabin kicked in and the house ransacked. The thieves had found their food stash but must have heard them coming because they only made off with a portion of it. Jupiter decided then that the area was becoming too dangerous for him and Kaya to stay. People were becoming desperate and desperate people were dangerous. He decided they would head for Nevada. He thought they'd be safer in the wilderness. Surely Black Rock City would be a gathering point of like-minded people, he had thought. The Burning Man would be the symbol of the new beginning instead of just a festival.

Her grandfather had built up such high hopes. But when they did finally reach the Black Rock Desert and the site of the festival, Kaya watched him crumble. When he had seen the playa deserted save a few shredded tents and a dusty car, he looked like a man defeated. They searched for the people but saw no other sign of them. So they went as far as they could, until the RV got stuck in the mud, and did what they had to do to survive in the arid desert.

Kaya liked the desert but it scared her. She felt like she was standing on a giant whale's back when she walked out alone, and at any moment it could dive down into the dark depths of the abyss. She felt that the desert had secrets, secrets that if she sat and listened long enough, it would tell her.

Jupiter joined her sometimes. In the evening they'd go for a walk and collect firewood, although Jupiter seemed to be getting weaker, having to stop for breaks more often. She chalked it up to malnutrition. It was on that last evening, the day before meeting Andrew, that Jupiter had been so quiet and distant. They were nearly out of food. A fact they were both aware of, but neither had mentioned it. Kaya felt like they had to do something but had been hoping that Jupiter would know what to do. It was apparent that he didn't. She felt the need to bring it up, but her heart raced at what the solution, or lack of one, might be.

"The food's almost gone," she said quietly. "We're going to die if we don't get out of here."

Jupiter hesitated a step, then kept going. He was silent for a long time, slowly walking along, gathering sticks for the fire. Kaya followed a few steps behind, doing the same. Finally, he took a deep breath and spoke.

"I know. I have something to tell you. I won't be able to go with you. I don't have the strength. I would slow you down too much. I... I have a cancer."

He paused, gauging her reaction. Kaya merely blinked. After a moment he continued.

"Too much smoke and chemicals in my younger days, I suppose. I'd probably be fine if I had just stuck with the pot.

But I don't think I have long. The last time I saw the doctor he said I had less than a year. That was fourteen months ago. Normally I would say that would be a good thing, but I can feel it, Kaya. It's growing inside me, spreading. I'm dying and you're going to have to survive on your own soon."

Kaya was shocked. Tears quivered at the edges of her eyes. She hadn't known her grandfather that well, but over the last few months they had bonded somewhat and she cared for the old man, despite his radical ways. She was scared, she couldn't be alone. She wouldn't know the first thing about surviving on her own. She started to say something; she wanted to, but the words didn't come. They wouldn't form right in her head, too much was spinning.

Andrew's arrival the following day had brought a distraction from what Jupiter had said, but she couldn't stop thinking about it. She had stayed in a somber mood, despite what was going on around her. Her grandfather was dying, and she would have no one left in this world.

She kicked a rock off the path and glanced up at the sagging sun. It would be dark soon. Andrew should be on his way back. If he found fuel that meant they would soon be leaving and she'd have to say goodbye. She didn't want to. Andrew had become familiar, and she was tired of leaving familiar behind. A spark of hope flashed in her chest. Maybe they could convince Andrew to come with them. They could go together and maybe find a community where there was a doctor who could help her grandfather.

Then the shadow of reality sank down and smothered the spark. Andrew couldn't come with them; he had family he was trying to find and the doctors had told Jupiter before that there was nothing they could do. Now after all this, there was surely nothing they could do.

She stopped at the top of a small hill and looked down at the valley to the south. She thought she could just make out a small dust trail rising from the horizon. It had to be Andrew, but he would be a while. She turned and glanced back towards camp. Squinting through the rays of the setting sun, she saw dust settling back at the camp. At first, she thought it was just the light playing tricks on her eyes, but then she heard angry shouting. She didn't think, she just ran.

When she could see the camp, her breath caught in her throat. There were four men with guns. Jupiter was screaming at them, telling them to go away. One of the men smashed the butt of his gun into Jupiter's face, doubling him over as a spray of crimson erupted from his nose. His hands desperately tried to hold back the pain and the blood gushing from his disfigured nose, but he dropped slowly to his knees as he listened to the man in front of him. The man, ignoring the rifle in his left hand, reached across his belt with his right and pulled a shiny pistol from its holster. He leveled it at Jupiter's head. He said something to him but Kaya's world was silent as she sprinted towards her grandfather. Jupiter turned his head and met Kaya's eyes, and in a look said 'goodbye'. She screamed as two flashes erupted from the tip of the pistol. Jupiter's body crumbled, falling back, and then was still.

The men raised their guns when they saw her, but she didn't care. One of the men grabbed her around the waist just before she reached her grandfather. She screamed and kicked but the man easily overpowered her, pinning her arms down.

"Well you are a pretty little thing aren't you?"

He was a fat, pockmarked, unshaven man, dirty in more ways than Kaya cared to count.

"Looks like we caught a good one Commander. Young and pretty."

He easily picked her up, dragging her over to the Humvee, snapping a set of handcuffs on her wrists before she could pull away. The man ran a rope through the handcuffs and tied her to the bumper of the vehicle. Kaya struggled and pulled, sobbing, barely able to breathe, as she watched the lifeless body of her grandfather.

The Commander pushed the grotesque man aside. A smile curled up on one side of his face that made Kaya wish she could shrink back and let the desert swallow her.

"Well little lady, the old man didn't tell me what I wanted to know, but I have a feeling you will."

CHAPTER 11
OLD FRIENDS

ANDREW DROVE off the side of the road and into a small wash as soon as he had seen the burning RV. He couldn't be sure but he was confident he wasn't spotted. He hopped off his bike and pulled his rifle from his back. He pulled the bolt back and with trembling hands bedded a round into the chamber. Ten rounds. He would need all of them. He'd have to aim carefully; the small bullets would only put a man down if placed in a vital area. He gripped the smooth wood stock of the rifle with sweaty palms. Blood pounded in his ears so loud that he wondered if he would even hear someone next to him. He jogged, back hunched, following the ravine as it curved around towards the campsite.

Andrew belly-crawled up the little hill that overlooked the camp, slowly inching his way to the top until he could see it. The roaring flames of the burning RV were almost too bright to look at. The vehicle still held its shape; the metal struts hadn't melted yet, but one side and the rear wall had burned away revealing the engulfing inferno inside. Andrew tore his eyes from the RV, hoping no one had been inside, and scanned the camp. Three men were watching the fire, all armed.

Andrew gasped, he could see Jupiter's body near the old campfire; his clothes were unmistakable. He tried not to look at the motionless body and continued to scan, desperate to find Kaya. Near the Humvee was another man. He thought this one looked to be the Commander, but he couldn't be sure in the fading light.

Then, he saw it, a small figure at the end of the Humvee, at the man's feet. *It* was Kaya. She was alive. She seemed to be tied to the bumper. Relief quickly turned to anger and Andrew ground his teeth.

What had they done to her?

He was ready to kill. But he needed a plan. He needed to get Kaya out of there. If he was lucky he could get two of them before they took cover and started firing back. Then he'd have no way of getting Kaya out and they might just kill her. He needed a distraction.

He worked his way back to the bike, unstrapping the plastic gas can, and then headed out into the darkness. He made sure to go far enough out across the flats that he wouldn't be spotted by the glow of the fire. Satisfied that he was in the right spot he loosened the cap and pulled out the flexible spout on the gas can. He backed up, working his way back to his bike as he poured a heavy trail of gas on the ground in a slow arc across the flats facing the campsite. When the can was empty, he dropped it and dug in his pocket until he found what he was looking for. He pulled the book of matches open and tore the first one free. He folded the cover back to pinch the match head and pulled. The head of the match erupted in a white and then blue flame. Carefully he slid the base of the match behind the rest of the matches and set the book down at the edge of the gas trail. He had seen it done in a movie once and hoped it would work as well as it had for Bruce Willis. He waited until he was satisfied that the match was going to keep burning and ran.

Andrew looked back just in time to see a ribbon of flame arc across the desert. He ran back to the top of the hill, knelt behind some brush and watched the men. They had seen the fire. It was hard to miss. Three men ran out to investigate but the fourth stayed near the Humvee. Andrew dropped back down and ran, working his way around to the hill beyond the Humvee.

He reached the next hill and could see Kaya curled up against the bumper and the Commander standing near her. His back was to him, watching the others running towards the fire. Andrew laid down in the prone position and put the sights of his rifle on the back of the man's head. He wasn't more than twenty yards away, an easy shot. If he was lucky, the roar of the still-burning RV would drown out the sound of the small caliber rifle. His heart hammered in his chest and the blood pounded in his head. His stomach felt sick. He held his breath and squeezed the trigger.

Andrew was up and running before the man hit the ground. Fueled by a surge of adrenaline, digging in his pocket, he pulled out his knife. He dropped to his knees when he reached Kaya and cut the rope that held her cuffed hands to the bumper. He grabbed her around the waist and hoisted her to her feet, gripping his rifle in one hand and her in the other. He looked down at the dead man. He could see the side of his face. The lifeless eyes weren't the Commander's.

They ran as fast as they could to the top of the hill and out of the light. Andrew stopped when they reached cover, dropped on one knee, and aimed back towards the camp. Something was running at him and Andrew fired without thinking. The man hunched into a ball clutching his stomach. Andrew fired again. This time he went limp and crumpled into the dirt.

Flashes appeared from behind the Humvee and the earth

around Andrew erupted. He turned and dove down the back side of the hill, away from the gunfire. Without stopping he grabbed Kaya and ran for the bike. Throwing his rifle over his shoulder as he jumped on, he then helped Kaya climb on behind him. He stuck his arm through her hands and then put them over his head so that she could hold on without choking him with the cuffs. He heeled back the kickstand and fired up the engine. His wrist gave the throttle two quick jerks and his foot kicked it down into gear. Spinning the bike around, he gunned it out into the flats.

He was almost to where he had lit the fire when he saw something step out in front of them. He thumbed on the headlight and the moment he did so, the Commander fired. Andrew swerved catching his balance, then pushed the throttle all the way open and roared towards the man. The Commander jumped away just as Andrew thought they were going to hit. He didn't stop, he didn't look back, he just kept the throttle twisted open as far as it would go. He switched the lights off so the taillight couldn't be seen and angled hard to the left to avoid the spray of gunfire that followed almost immediately.

"How can you see?!" screamed Kaya.

"I can't! Don't worry it should be flat for miles."

"What about rocks?"

Andrew didn't answer but strained his eyes as hard as he could to see in front of them. Suddenly the moonlit flats were interrupted by a head-sized rock ten feet straight in front of them. He swerved to the right, but he was still unused to the weight of a passenger. He went over further than he expected. He leaned back to the left trying to correct it and started to lose control.

Suddenly, Kaya realizing what was happening, pulled herself tight to Andrew, leaning with him. Andrew pressed forward hard on the handlebars trying to stop it from wobbling. Finally, it smoothed out.

Andrew could feel Kaya's head buried in his back. She was sobbing. His heart ached for her but there wasn't anything he could do about it now. He had to get them to safety. When they reached the edge of the flats, Andrew turned north, following the base of the mountains, the way Lee had said to.

After a while, the bike lurched over a bump and suddenly they were back on a dirt road. Just as he was starting to pick up speed, Andrew felt the engine cough. A red light started flashing next to his speedometer. He could smell smoke and something sweet. He squinted at the gauges. The engine temperature was redlining. In an instant, he knew what happened.

He felt the engine cough again and this time it died. He quickly pulled in the clutch and squeezed the brake. Easing to a stop in the gravel. Steam was rolling up and out of the front of the bike. Andrew cursed. He unwound himself from Kaya's shaking arms and slid off the bike. He surveyed the front of the bike. In the faint light of the moon, he could see a tiny trickle of coolant pooling on the ground and a small black hole in the middle of the radiator and he knew they were now on foot.

"Come on," he said. "We've got to get up into the hills, the bike is shot. We'll have to walk from here."

"What? How? What will we do? Where will we go? They'll find us and kill us..." Kaya's voice cracked and she began to break.

"I'm not going to let that happen. We can get up into the hills where they can't follow us unless they are on foot too. We can outrun them and we can hide. We can make our way to my uncle's ranch. We'll be safe. But we have to go now. Come on, let me help you off."

Andrew grabbed her around her waist and she threw her cuffed hands over his head as he lifted her. She slid her leg over the seat and once off the bike, she hugged him tightly.

"Thank you," she whispered.

Andrew lost in the embrace, took almost a full second to register the distant headlights coming their way.

"Time to go."

———

Andrew's thighs throbbed as he sprinted up the hill. He had his guns, the pistol his father had given him, and the rifle Lee had given him. He had a one-liter aluminum bottle of gasoline taken from the bike, and he had Kaya. They would have to hunt and they would have to find water, but he couldn't think about that now. They had to get to safety, wherever that might be.

Kaya was struggling to keep up, her hands banded together by the handcuffs made running awkward. Andrew stopped to allow her to catch up. He sucked in a gulp of air trying to cool his burning lungs. He glanced back down the hill. The headlights had almost reached the bike, they had to move faster.

"Are you alright?" he asked.

"Yeah... I'm... okay." she managed, through gasping breaths.

"If we can make it up into the rocks, we can find cover and be able to watch if they're coming up. But we have got to keep moving."

"Okay. I can do it."

Andrew nodded and started the steep ascent again. The muscles in his calves and thighs quivered from fatigue. All he wanted to do was lie down and pass out. He pushed the thoughts aside and instead focused on the dim outline of the rocky outcrop above him. He leaned forward into the climb and walked on the balls of his feet, barely letting his heels touch the ground.

Andrew turned to see where their pursuers were. They

had stopped just short of the bike, bathing it with a spotlight. The light turned, shining across the desert and then over the hillside.

Andrew and Kaya, confident they couldn't be seen, being well above where the lights were shining, stood and watched for a moment. Andrew hoped the men thought they had gone back across the salt flats. The Humvee didn't move for a long time, then the lights went out and Andrew heard the thump of a car door closing. They were coming.

They had to find some sort of cover before morning or else they'd be sitting ducks. The high-caliber rifles the men carried could pick them off from distances much further than Andrew's small rifle could reach. He glanced down at Kaya. She was sitting on a rock and looked exhausted. They couldn't keep up this pace, not on a hill this steep. He looked back down the hill. The hillside was barely visible in the dim moonlight. He couldn't see the men, but that meant they couldn't see him and Kaya either. They'd be making their way slowly.

Pretty tough to track someone in the dark.

For all they knew Andrew and Kaya could be hiding anywhere on this hillside, so they'd spread out and try to listen. He smiled. For the first time, he had the advantage over the Commander, and he planned on keeping it that way. If they could just make it to high ground where they could hide and wait for the Commander to get close, he'd have him. He thought he could see some sort of a ledge a ways above them.

As good a place as any.

"Come on Kaya. We're close." He pulled her up and held her. "Almost there."

He kept his arm around her and guided her up the steep grade. He glanced back every so often, but never saw or heard anything. They trekked on for what seemed like hours, the ledge moving as they moved, like a mirage, just out of reach. Sweat poured out from under his fur-lined hat. He stopped to wipe his brow and cursed it. He was grateful for it in the cold and would be again once he stopped and his body temperature dropped, but for now, he was ready to throw it to the wolves. He sighed and pulled it back down on his head.

Andrew stopped suddenly, aware that he was standing on flat ground. The ground was flat for about two feet then the steep slope started up again. He turned a circle examining the platform, his chest still heaving from the climb. This wasn't ideal, but it might just work, he thought. They could sit here and wait for the light to come, and then be able to shoot down at the Commander. But there was the problem of the Commander and the other man being out of range of his small rifle. Then once they spotted him and Kaya, they'd be pinned. His exhaustion was getting the better of him, he wasn't thinking clearly.

"Wait here," he said.

Andrew stepped to the left. The area was much wider than he had assumed, in fact, it just kept going. He followed it for twenty or thirty feet, it was easily two to three feet wide the whole way and packed hard as asphalt. He returned when he heard Kaya calling for him.

"Sorry," he said.

"I was exploring. I think this is a trail. Lee told me one time that bighorn sheep make trails that are like highways on the high hillsides. They are wide enough that the sheep can't be seen from below and they can travel the whole length of the range. I think that's what this is. It's flat and easygoing; we can be long gone before they even get here. Do you think you can keep going for a while?"

"I think so. But I could use some water."

"I know, me too. We'll have to try to find some in the morning. Are you ready?"

She stood without a word and waited; her head high and

her shoulder's back, and Andrew witnessed her most attractive quality. He had seen glimpses before, but he was struck by it now. She had lost her parents and her grandfather, the only people she had in this world, and now was running for her life. At the point of exhaustion, she was still standing tall, fighting. A beautiful strength that sent a flutter through Andrew's chest. He was feeling something for her he had never felt before.

He smiled, grabbed her hand, and led her down the path. In the back of his mind, Andrew was struggling with what had just taken place. He had killed two men. It had to happen, but the reality of it stuck in his heart like a blade. Two men were no longer in this world, because of him. It had been easy, easier than it should have been. In the heat of the moment, he had done what he had to, to save Kaya. He hadn't had time to think. Now that he did, his stomach felt like he was on a roller coaster. He did his best to push the feelings aside and focus on the trail.

The going was slow; he had to look hard to see the trail ahead, careful not to allow himself or Kaya to step off the path. Doing so would mean falling, probably to their death. The hillside had turned into a cliff, they wouldn't have known it except that he had kicked a rock off the side and heard it hit the bottom several seconds later. Kaya kept tight to him, mimicking his every step. As the moon rose higher, it got easier. Andrew was able to see further and they developed a steady pace. After nearly an hour, in a sleepy stupor, they decided to stop. They climbed up the hill a ways so they wouldn't be on the trail in case their pursuers stumbled on it.

Above them was an outcropping of rocks. When they reached it they found a flat spot that curved back into the rocks. Andrew kicked the worst of the rocks out of the way, smoothing out the dirt, and helped Kaya sit down against the wall.

He walked back to the edge looking down the trail and

was satisfied that they wouldn't be seen if someone happened to walk by. He slumped down against the rock next to Kaya. He wanted to put his arm around her, but fear paralyzed him. He started to say something but stopped. Finally, heart hammering, he lifted his arm and put it around her. It felt like slow motion. But the moment he did, she embraced it and snuggled in next to him, tilting her head on his shoulder. He felt a warmth rush over him that nearly made him break into a sweat in the cold autumn night.

"Did you see what they did to him?" she whispered.

He could feel her body quiver a little and he thought he could see tears in her eyes.

"Yes," he answered. "I'm sorry. Try not to think about it. Try to get some sleep."

She laid her head into the crook of his neck and rested her hands on his thigh. Andrew stared out at the stars; there were patches of darkness where clouds covered the sky. He didn't know what tomorrow was going to bring, they might be killed, but what he did know was that there was no other place in the world that he would rather be right now.

CHAPTER 12
RUDE AWAKENINGS

ANDREW'S EYES blinked the sleep away, and he took in the gray misty morning. Dawn had brought a light rain. Small drops hung from the rock ledge a few feet above their heads. He looked down at Kaya. She was still curled up against him with her head on his chest. He had to move, sitting all night against the rock made his body stiff and sore. His legs ached to stretch, but he didn't.

I think I'd let a snake bite me before I'd move from this spot.

He stared down at her soft, beautiful, dreaming face. He smiled and leaned back against the rock. His eyes scanned the horizon. There were cells of scattered downpours he could see, spread across the desert, but most were miles away.

She stirred a little but her head stayed resting on his chest. He felt her shiver a little and he wrapped his arm around her small shoulders. This time when she stirred, her eyes flickered open. He looked down into them and smiled.

"Good morning."

She sat up quickly and pulled away, as if surprised.

"Oh, uh, good morning."

"You alright?" he asked.

"Yes, fine."

"Okay, then."

He was confused by her reaction, but at this point, all that mattered was standing up. He stood and then bent over, reaching for his feet. His muscles felt exhilarated to be free of their imprisoned position.

Ahh, like a cold glass of water to a man dying of thirst. Which, ironically is something we don't have, or food for that matter, he thought.

Food and water would have to wait. He crept up onto a rock and surveyed the trail. No sign of them, but he could only see a few hundred yards of the trail before it curved back around the hillside. He hoped they had given up and gone home, but he knew better. The Commander had come back for him. He was hunting him, but why? Why was he still pursuing him? Could it be because he was the only survivor? The only witness to the massacre of his hometown? Why would it matter?

He shook his head. He had no idea why. Andrew exhaled deeply, trying to push away his frustrations. As he breathed in he took in the aroma of the wet sagebrush, his favorite smell.

If only this were the old days and me and Kaya were here on a camping trip; cooking by the campfire, exploring the hot springs. Oh well, what's the point of an adventure if there's no danger of death?

He shook his head, not liking his train of thought, and jumped from the rock to return to Kaya. He was pleasantly surprised at the scene before him. She was doing some sort of stretch. Feet on the ground, legs angled, her body bent at the hips, back straight, still cuffed hands flat on the ground, her body forming a triangle. He crossed his arms and watched.

She stood, straightening her back and stretching her arms upward, seeming not to notice his ogling. Finally, she let her arms down and let out a long breath. She eyed him, and immediately he averted his eyes, knowing he'd been caught staring. He uncrossed his arms and shifted nervously.

"Um, what.. uh, are you doing?"

"It's called down-facing dog."

She waited a moment to gauge his reaction. A confused expression fixed on his face. She smirked, happy to have stumped him.

"It's a yoga pose."

It sounded snootier than she had intended and she quickly tried to cover it.

"I could teach you a few poses if you want."

"Maybe some other time. We need to get moving. I want to run back and check to see if they are on the trail behind us. As long as they aren't, we can just keep following the trail to the north and they'll probably never find us up here."

"And if they are?"

"Then we'll have to do something about it. I don't know what, but we can't keep running like this, especially without food or water. I'll be back in a minute."

"Okay."

He smiled and set off in a lope down the trail. Light drops of mist hit him in the face. He knew what he had to do. He knew he had to kill these men, like the two he killed the day before. His jaw clenched at the memory of what he had done. He didn't like it, but he knew he had to do it. The Commander would just keep coming. He'd chase them until either he or Andrew was dead and Andrew knew it.

The rifle rested in both hands as he jogged. His hat wobbled on his head at the pace. He was once again glad for its warmth on the cool misty morning.

Andrew slowed down when he reached where the trail disappeared around the bend of the hill. He crept forward, scanning the next hillside as it came into view. He stopped when he knew most of his body would still be concealed and squatted down. His eyes panned across the steep hill, looking for any sign of movement, any out-of-place color or shadow, anything that didn't belong. He crept forward some more, taking in more of the hillside. No movement, no sounds, nothing. He wasn't sure if he was relieved or upset about it. From where he was he had at least a two-mile-wide, panorama view of the next hillside.

The uneasiness in his gut gnawed at him. Andrew knew the Commander wouldn't have given up, but he thought they would have been closer by now. He was about to stand and jog to the next bend when something caught his eye. On the next hillside, far below him, just coming around into view there was something. He lay down on his stomach at the edge of the trail and squinted, trying to see clearer. It was them, it had to be; two figures moving along at an upward angle towards his position. They had to be nearly a mile away. Coming uphill, it was going to take them a while. Obviously, they had not climbed high enough to find the trail, yet.

Andrew sat back and allowed himself to close out the world, to think. He needed a plan. Right now he had three advantages: he knew where they were, they didn't know where he was, and they had to climb uphill to get to him. He had to start thinking like a hunter. They were his prey. He looked up the hill. They weren't far from the tree line. There were a few small pines and scrub brushes scattered around near where he sat. He thought he should try to use the cover of the trees to his advantage, as well.

What would Lee tell me to do?

Set a trap.

Okay. What kind of a trap?

––––––

Kaya fed the flames of the fire with twisted branches of sagebrush and dead pine. The fire popped and sparked. The greasy smoke rose into the cloudy sky. She rubbed at her sore wrists, finally relieved of the handcuffs after Andrew had spent more than twenty minutes picking them with the blade of his pocketknife and a bit of the zipper from his coat.

She was nervous. She knew the men were coming, men who killed her grandfather, men who had beaten her, men she never wanted to see again. But she trusted Andrew, she knew he would keep her safe, he would protect her. She found herself thinking about Andrew more than normal, perhaps to help keep her from thinking of Jupiter. But Andrew was there; a presence that made her heart race when he was around and her mind race when he wasn't. The way he smiled when he teased her, or when he knew he was right about something. The way his unkempt hair fell into his light brown eyes when he wasn't wearing his silly fur hat. The way he would hold out his hand to help her. She liked that. Spending the night in his arms had been wonderful; she wasn't sure why she acted the way she did that morning. She had felt embarrassed but she couldn't figure out why.

She hadn't ever really dated anyone and was at a loss about how she should act. She wished she had someone to talk to, one of her friends from school maybe. Megan and Shawna would have known what she should do. They would have giggled and teased her to no end, but they would have offered some form of guidance. She wondered if either of them was still alive, she doubted it. Not many survived. She shivered, remembering the piles of body bags stacked out in the parking lot of the hospital because there was nowhere else to put them. Then her parents...

She pushed the images from her mind and gazed into the flames as they licked the air, like the darting tongue of a snake. She longed for something to call home. She was a homeless orphan with nowhere to go. Being with Andrew did make things feel better.

He feels a little like home.

A large raindrop sizzled when it landed on a glowing

piece of charcoal. She looked up at the sky. The clouds were high and gray. More rain would come but no dark heavy clouds could be seen to threaten a downpour. She felt a drop land on her neck, it was a shock but not unpleasant. Like kisses on her skin. She smiled, her mind once again drifting to Andrew.

He had told her to wait until he signaled, keeping the fire fed. Then she was supposed to place the aluminum canister of fuel that he had taken from the bike next to the fire. Then as soon as she spotted the men, she was supposed to run up the hill to a group of rocks to hide until he came for her. The men might follow her but Andrew said that he would stop them. She knew the plan but she was nervous and hated waiting. She had been sitting here, feeding the flames for what seemed like hours, and was beginning to worry.

What if Andrew has been injured, or worse, attacked by the commander? He might need me.

She took a deep breath; she was letting her emotions feed her imagination. She must wait here. Andrew was depending on her. She was hungry and that wasn't helping either. It had been nearly twenty-four hours since she had had anything to eat. The smell of the smoke reminded her of the cooking fire and her stomach growled in impatience. She tossed another chunk onto the fire, sending embers and dark smoke into the air, and stared across the gray horizon framed by the crooked pines.

———

Andrew watched the men climb the hill from his perch amongst the brush and trees. They had seen the smoke and were making their way towards it slowly. His timing had to be perfect or else Kaya would be in danger. He didn't like putting her in harm's way, but this was the only way he could see this working. The trees narrowed where she was. To pursue her they would have to run right past the fire. That was his window. If he missed, it was lost and he'd probably only be able to take down one of them before they reached Kaya. They had to spot her in order to chase after her, running past the fire and the canister. If they didn't, they would be cautious, and not go near the fire until they found out where he and Kaya were.

The two men reached the boulder Andrew had chosen as his marker. It was time. He made his way to his other perch off to his right, above Kaya and the fire. He could no longer see the men, but he had a view of the way they'd have to come. It wouldn't be long now. He picked up a rock to throw and alert Kaya. He was about to throw it when he heard a branch break off to the left. He spun but the man kicked his rifle aside as he landed on top of him, punching him, hit after hit. Andrew struggled to fight back but the man overpowered him. He bucked and kicked but the man had his arms pinned with his knees, leaving Andrew no way to block the relentless barrage of flashing fists landing on his cheekbones. He heard a scream and knew it was Kaya. His heart raged inside, he closed his eyes to block out the pain. He had to save her.

With a rush of desperation, he kicked up as hard and as fast as he could. He felt the muscles in his hamstring flex further than they were ever supposed to flex, but he also felt a satisfying thump as the tip of his boot caught the man in the back of the head, sending him sprawling. Andrew tried to stand up but his leg erupted in an explosion of pain. He fell clutching the back of his thigh.

The man regained himself and went for his rifle leaning against a tree. Andrew looked around frantically for his own rifle. As soon as he spotted it, he rolled to it snatching it up. He took aim and fired, hitting the man in the chest. The man clutched his breast but kept moving towards his weapon. Just as he reached his gun, Andrew fired again and a small dark hole materialized at the man's temple. The man died as his knees hit the ground.

Andrew struggled to get up, but his leg wouldn't hold his weight. He hobbled to the edge overlooking the fire. Kaya was struggling with the Commander; he slapped her hard, but she fought back. Andrew's mind raced. He couldn't shoot the Commander, for fear of hitting Kaya. He looked at the fire. She had done it, the canister was in place. They weren't close to the fire, but maybe it would be enough of a distraction that Kaya could get away.

He didn't hesitate, he aimed and fired. The small lead bullet punched through the aluminum skin of the canister, spinning through the fluid and exiting the other side, sending out a fine mist of gasoline across the flames of the fire, erupting into a fireball in less than a second. As the explosion occurred, the Commander turned and Kaya broke free, running for the trees. He turned back and pursued her. Andrew frantically chambered another round and fired at the Commander just before he disappeared into the trees. He couldn't tell if he had hit him. He pushed himself up and tried to pursue them but fell, the muscles in his leg burning like fire. He pushed himself back up and heard a scream. He held his breath. *Kaya.* Then he heard a shot. His heart froze.

"Kaya!"

He struggled to get up, making it a few more feet before falling again. Tears blurred his eyes. The air left his lungs. He struggled to draw a breath. He lay there sobbing, but gripped his gun tight and waited for the Commander to appear. He would kill him. He would kill the bastard for what he had done.

———

The explosion startled her; but the moment she saw the Commander turn and felt his grip slacken, she tore free and ran. Her heart raced, every part of her conscious mind screamed at her to run for the trees. Her feet pounded the dirt but she couldn't feel her legs. She pushed harder than she had ever pushed before. It got darker as she made it into the trees, reaching a large rock, and started to climb. She could feel the Commander coming, like a knife about to slash her back. She had made it halfway up the rock when her foot slipped. All of her weight came down, held only by her fingertips; the rocky ledge tore through the pads of her fingers as she fell. A scream echoed out of her lungs as she landed on her foot and felt her ankle pop.

She tried to get up but the Commander was there rushing at her. Her hand slid inside her coat and pulled out Andrew's pistol, leveling the barrel at the Commander. He stopped, holding up his rifle in mock surrender, as a smile curled up his lip.

"Okay, okay you got me. We don't want to hurt you. We just want to talk. What's your name, little lady?"

Kaya slid down the safety with her thumb, just like Andrew had shown her. She aimed down the barrel, just like he had shown her. The Commander's smile faded and he started to say something else as he took a step forward. Kaya's finger squeezed the trigger, just like Andrew had shown her.

A crimson mist erupted as the bullet left the Commander's head and he fell to the ground. Kaya sucked in air, breathing for the first time since she had pulled the gun from her jacket. She sobbed in between heavy gasps, tears leaving streaks down her soiled face, her body shaking uncontrollably. She was devastated by what she had done. The man whose life she had just ended had taken her grandfather's not twenty-four hours before. The reality of all that this meant sent her head spinning and made her nauseous. She choked on her gasping cries, vomiting her shame and fear next to the man she had killed, giving up what little was left in her stomach.

After a time, she remembered Andrew, shocked that he hadn't come yet. Her mind filled with images of him bleeding, dying, while she sat here, crying. She forced herself up and tried putting weight on her ankle. It hurt like hell. She couldn't tell if it was broken. It didn't matter if it was, she had to find Andrew. She limped from tree to tree, using each as a support, desperate to find him.

———

Andrew watched, waiting for the Commander to come out. He would kill him before he had a chance to spot Andrew. Laid out next to a rock with his gun propped up, Andrew waited. He rubbed at his tearing eyes, holding back the pain as much as he could. He had to keep it together until it was over. He had to do it for Kaya. He wiped his nose with the back of his sleeve.

Finally, he spotted movement and prepared himself. He could see him moving through the trees. Andrew watched, waiting for the clear shot. His finger wiped the sweat off the trigger and settled back into place. The open metal sights lined up on him, moving through the trees into the clearing. Just as the figure appeared, his finger started to squeeze.

"Andrew!"

Kaya?

He immediately pulled his finger away from the trigger and clicked on the safety. Andrew struggled to stand, but his whole body was shaking. He couldn't believe what he had almost done.

"Kaya, I'm here!"

Andrew used the rock to push himself up. He winced in pain as he tried to take a step but forced himself forward.

"Andrew!"

Kaya limped to him as fast as she could, her ankle swelling with each painful step. When she reached him she threw her arms around him and pulled him in tight. After a moment she pulled back.

"What happened?" asked Kaya.

"I think I tore a muscle. What about you? What happened? I thought you were..."

"I tried to climb to the rock but I fell on my ankle."

"What about the Commander?"

Kaya hesitated; despair filled her eyes with tears once again. Andrew understood. He pulled her in tight, stroking the back of her hair as she sobbed into his chest.

"It's alright," he told her. "You did what you had to do."

It was all he could say, all he could do. He knew it didn't help. He knew the empty, hollow, sickening feeling that came from taking another life and he wished he could take that empty feeling away from her. He wished he had been the one to do it. He wished he could carry the burden of guilt for her, but he couldn't. All he could do was hold her while she wept.

CHAPTER 13
NOT JUST THE WIND HOWLS

ANDREW AND KAYA slowly made their way further up into the mountains and further away from the memory of death. They found a downed tree that created a bit of a small shelter beneath its dead branches and decided to stop for the night. They huddled together in the darkness, gripping each other trying to keep warm. Both were exhausted and hungry. The day's events played like a grainy horror film in their heads. There was a numbness that shrouded their memories in a fog; the mind's own safeguard, stemming from the mix of the trauma, shock, and exhaustion.

Andrew could hear Kaya's teeth chattering. He had nothing to start a fire with. The way the wind howled down the mountain, he doubted he could start one anyway. He pulled off his fur hat and put it on her, tying down the warm ear flaps beneath her chin. She halfheartedly smiled at him and nuzzled her head into his neck. His now exposed ears ached in the icy wind, but the warmth from Kaya made the cold much more bearable. He pulled her in tight and they prepared themselves for a night of fitful sleep there beneath the fallen tree, on the side of a cold and windy mountain.

Just as Andrew's eyelids began to close, he thought he

heard something more than just the wind's howling. He tried to listen but the call of sleep and his heavy eyelids convinced him it was just the wind.

————

Andrew woke just after dawn, the icy wind still blasting his face. His stiff body yearned to move but the warmth coming from Kaya was almost too comforting to abandon. Finally, the need to reposition his injured leg forced him up. He eased himself away from Kaya so as not to wake her. He felt weak and unrested as he pushed himself to his, slowly letting his injured leg take his weight.

Winter was coming. They needed to get off the mountain, but more so, they needed food and water. He wished he had been able to snag his duffel bag of food before they had fled. They hadn't seen any sign of game, but then again they had been running, not hunting.

His leg still ached when he tried to straighten it and he could feel the muscles in his chest and arms sore from his struggle the day before. Andrew rubbed up and down his leg as hard as he could, kneading his hamstring and calf then stood and stretched his back. He felt wrecked between his sore muscles, his fatigue, and his hunger.

A hot shower and a hot breakfast sure would be nice right about now... yeah sure, maybe a room at the Ritz and a deep tissue massage, too. Good luck with that.

The air from his lungs slowly hissed past his lips as he exhaled. The events of yesterday played back in his mind. Kaya had done it, she had killed the Commander. His guilt returned. He should have been the one to do it. He shouldn't have put her in that position. It was stupid and reckless and because of it, she had to take a life.

Kaya stirred and Andrew was pulled back to the present.

"Good morning," he said softly.

"Morning."

Her voice was hoarse and quiet. There was little color in her face and her eyes held a distant, expressionless gaze. She sat up, hugging herself and shivering.

"It's so cold."

"I know. Sun will be up soon. We'll start making our way down today. It'll be warmer once we get off this mountain."

"That's good. If you don't mind, I need to use the bathroom."

"Oh okay, I'll uh... I'll go down the hill a ways. See if I can find us something to eat."

Andrew picked up his rifle and shoved his free hand into the warmth of his pocket. He meandered a ways down the hillside, limping along slowly, scanning the trees for any sign of movement. This was when game should be moving around, leaving their beds to find food and warm sunshine to stand in. Without binoculars or a scope of some kind, it would be difficult to spot anything more than two or three hundred yards away, especially if it wasn't moving. He tried to recall what Lee had told him about spotting game.

Scan slowly across the terrain, let your eyes relax, and don't strain. Your eyes will instinctively pick out anything that doesn't fit, a shadow where it shouldn't be, a glimmer of sunlight on fur, a slight movement. Your eyes will catch it, but your brain may not. So you have to relax and let your eyes go where they want, then focus on the areas they're drawn to. If there's anything out there, you'll spot it.

He was grateful to the old mountain man. He had taught him a lot and he hoped desperately that the Commander had not gone back to his small cabin before finding them, but with a sickening feeling in his gut, he knew that was unlikely.

Andrew noticed a flock of large birds in a tree a few hundred yards away. He was about to investigate when he heard Kaya approaching. He turned and looked. She was moving slowly, limping.

"How's the ankle?"

A stupid question he realized after he had asked it, but she didn't attack it.

"Sore. It made peeing difficult that's for sure."

She laughed a bit, but there was little cheer in her voice.

"You want me to take a look at it? Here, have a seat."

Kaya sat at the base of a tree and pulled up her pant leg. Andrew knelt and untied her shoe and tried to ease it off her foot pulling at the heel, but it was tight. Kaya grimaced from the pain as he pulled, and then the shoe suddenly slipped off. She groaned as she felt the release of the pressure in her ankle.

Andrew could see even before he removed her soiled sock that her foot was badly swollen. As he slipped it off, it revealed a nasty bruise on the outside of her ankle. He held her foot gingerly examining the tender joint. He slowly swiveled her foot around, listening and feeling for anything that might mean a break. The look on her face told him she was in pain, but if it was broken she'd be screaming or hitting him with whatever she could reach.

"It's bad, but I don't think it's broken. But we aren't going to be hiking very far until that heals up unless I can find something to make some sort of a splint with. It was probably stupid to take your shoe off, but I wanted to know it wasn't broken. I doubt now we'd be able to get it back on though, at least until the swelling goes down."

Kaya sat silently while Andrew slipped her sock back on as carefully as possible. Andrew could see her hands were shaking. Finally, she spoke softly, her voice almost cracking.

"What are we going to do now?"

She spoke again before he could answer.

"We're both hurt; we can't get off this mountain. Winter is coming, and we are going to starve to death if we don't freeze to death first."

The tears dropped down to her trembling lips. Andrew pulled a leaf from her hair and smiled.

"Well first, I am going to find us some food and water. Then we are going to build some kind of shelter to stay in until we can hike off this mountain. Then we are going to make it to my uncle's ranch."

Andrew wiped her tears and stroked her face. They looked into each other's eyes for a moment. They both felt it, the fear, the exposure, the vulnerability, the need to look away, but at the same time the connection. A dimple formed at the side of his mouth revealing a hint of a smile. She smiled too.

"You always know what to say..."

His heart pounded as she bit her lip and her hand reached up to his neck and slowly pulled him to her. She tilted her head up towards his as he closed his eyes and met her with his lips. His hand pushed through her hair, his fingers combing through her tangles to the back of her neck, pulling himself further into her kiss. Her hand stroked his face, down his neck, and came to rest on his chest.

She lay back onto the pine needles, pulling him with her. He used his hand to hold himself up, worried that his weight might hurt her. The tension in his arm and the excitement of the moment caused his arm to quiver uncontrollably. His other hand slowly left the back of her neck, his callused fingers drawing an arc down the side of her neck slowly, hesitantly.

Fear caused his hand to stop. His head swimming, he pulled away from her lips to catch his breath. They stared once again into one another's eyes. Each feeling a need, a hunger, an excitement that was blocked only by the fear of uncertainty.

Kaya let out a deep breath and smiled. Her hand grasped the back of his neck and pulled him down, their lips embracing once again. His hand, now more confident, edged slowly down the neckline of her shirt and came to rest, softly cupping her breast. He felt her give a small gasp and he started to pull away, but she held tight to the back of his head. Her hips rose to meet his, wanting, needing to be closer. As they gave in to their own desires, they both forgot for a short while about their plight, the dangers, and the loved ones left behind. As they experienced one another for the first time, they felt complete.

————

It was the afternoon of a late autumn day as Andrew leaned against a rock overlooking the hillside below. This had been one of the most wonderful days he had experienced. He had been with a girl for the first time, a girl that he loved and cared for. Kaya could be difficult and at times he didn't know how to act around her, but when they had been together it had felt right and her touch was something that sent electricity through his body. He struggled to form simple sentences when she was close, his heart hammering so loud in his ear that he couldn't hear himself think.

Now as he sat on the rock staring down at the disfigured body below him, he thought that this day could possibly turn into one of the worst. In their state of bliss, they had blocked out the world. A temporary reprieve from the trying horrors they had faced, a vacation of the spirit. Now awakened from his stupor, he realized how dangerous it was to let his guard down.

He had thought they could finally relax and enjoy some peace now that the Commander was dead and they were no longer being hunted. But in the night, the bodies of the two men had been mutilated by a threat just as dangerous as the Commander. As soon as he had seen the tracks, he knew. It wasn't just the wind that had been howling last night, it was a wolf.

Earlier in the day Andrew had gone to look for food and water. He had managed to find a spring in a small ravine. He had dropped on all fours and drank greedily until his stomach ached. When he could drink no more, he thought of Kaya, and how he was going to get water to her. With her swollen ankle, there would be no way she could make the hike into the ravine, and he had found nothing he could carry water with. He walked in an outward spiral away from the spring looking for anything he could use.

He came upon a grove of Aspen trees and noticed large pieces of the paper-like bark lying about. He gathered a few of the larger pieces and tried to form them into a cup, but as he folded, cracks formed and they broke into pieces. Finally, he gave up and moved on. He hiked around for another half-hour but found nothing that would work. He came back to the spring and stared at the cold, life-giving water, his hand resting on the empty holster on his hip. Kaya still had his pistol; he wanted to make sure she had it anytime he was away. He looked down at his belt.

Idiot.

Andrew tore off his belt and removed the holster. It was leather and stitched tight up the side, a perfect cup. He dipped it into the water, filling it to the brim. He held it up and waited, watching for a leak. Water dripped off the side, but it slowed and finally stopped.

"Good enough."

He walked back to their camp, doing his best not to spill it. Kaya had watched him as he made his way slowly back to her, holding something up, and puzzled at what he was up to. Laughing at his odd behavior, she finally called out to him.

"What the heck are you doing?"

"Bringing you a surprise!"

"Ooh. What is it?"

"It wouldn't be a very good surprise if I told you! Be patient."

"I've been watching you tiptoe for ten minutes! A girl only has so much patience!"

"Just a minute longer."

Finally, he stood before her and bent over, handing her the holster. Her eyes widened when she saw the contents.

"Water? Thank you, thank you, thank you!"

She drank the water down in three gulps, wiping her face with the back of her hand when she was done.

"Oh, that's good," she sighed. "Tastes a little like leather though."

"Jeez, that's gratitude. Last time I bring you a surprise," said Andrew smiling.

"You're right. I'm sorry. Leather water is definitely better than no water."

She batted her eyelashes and mustered the sweetest smile that she could.

"Could I please have some more leather water?"

"Only if you're nice."

He pinched her side.

"Hey, that hurt!"

He snickered as he snatched up the holster and made his way back to the spring.

"Bully!"

Andrew waved without turning around. He filled the holster twice more for her and when she was satisfied he filled it again so they had it with them. He left it leaning against a tree to keep it from spilling. Sitting next to her, he stretched out his leg and massaged the aching muscle. Kaya laid her hand across his thigh and looked at him with pity.

"Does it hurt bad?"

"I'll live, I suppose. I've got to go see if I can find us some food."

He wrapped his arm around her, his hand resting on her waist.

"How's your foot? Has the swelling gone down?"

"A little," she said, grinned mischievously. "It doesn't exactly help when we go rolling around in the leaves."

"Oh... did I hurt you? I didn't mean to..."

A look of horror crossed his face, but her laughs cut him off.

"No, I'm fine! I'm just teasing you."

Softer, she said into his ear, "Actually I enjoyed that very much."

She kissed his neck and then nibbled on his ear. The air left his body and his head felt light. She kissed his cheek following his jawline; he turned his head and met her lips. He wrapped his arms around her and pulled her to him, but as he did so her foot twisted and she screamed out in pain.

"Shoot. Sorry. Are you alright?"

Kaya sat up rubbing her ankle, her teeth clenched. She said nothing for a moment, just rubbing the swollen joint.

"Mmhm, I'm alright. That's just *really* painful. I'll be okay though. What I wouldn't give for an aspirin right now."

"Sorry. I think I better go try to find us some food and maybe build some sort of shelter before it gets dark."

"Okay. I'll just wait here then."

Andrew raised an eyebrow at her and she smirked.

"I'll be back as quick as I can," he said as he set off down the hill.

He hoped he hadn't hurt her, but she seemed alright. She was amazing and he was in love, or at least thought he was. He smiled to himself; and if it hadn't been for his tender leg, he might have skipped.

Andrew had been walking along for nearly ten minutes lost in thought, when he remembered what he was supposed to be doing. He was hunting, scavenging, and grazing for anything that would keep them alive. He had his rifle and could bring down anything smaller than a deer but if he saw one, he definitely wouldn't pass it up. That much venison would keep them fed easily until they could travel again.

The problem was he hadn't seen any fresh sign, let alone an actual animal. He had seen a few hoof prints at the spring but they were dried up and most likely weeks old. He hadn't seen any sort of animal in the area except for a few chipmunks and a flock of small black birds flying overhead. He could feel his body getting weaker, he felt exhausted just from the short downhill hike. He would take whatever animal he could get.

That was when he spotted the tree full of birds again and remembered seeing them that morning. He was close to where they had fought the Commander and his goon. He realized the birds were probably attracted by the smell of death. Suddenly the thought of eating birds that might have been eating human flesh turned his empty stomach into knots. Still, they had maybe one more day before finding food was a matter of life or death, and every hour that passed meant the hunt would be that much more difficult.

He crept closer, keeping low under the brush. He chose his path carefully, avoiding twigs and dry leaves to avoid alerting the birds. He checked his rifle, making sure the magazine was in tight and checking to make sure there was a round in the chamber by drawing back the bolt until he saw the shiny brass casing.

Andrew climbed the rock ahead of him overlooking the clearing, sliding to his belly in a prone position. He propped the gun up in his hand, resting his cheek on the cold wood grain of the stock. He aimed, lining up the sights on the largest concentration of birds. He knew that after the first shot, they'd scatter, leaving him with maybe one bird. He decided to squeeze off as many shots into the group as he could before they all flew.

As he aimed at a fat one in the cluster, he winced at the thought of what the bird must have been gorging itself on. He fired, chambered another round, fired again, chambered again, and managed to get off a third shot as birds and feathers flew everywhere in a screeching black cloud. He watched as at least two birds hit the ground.

Good.

Better than he had hoped. He picked himself up off the rock and rubbed away the small pebbles that had stuck to him. He made his way back down and around the rock to collect his prize. He had a spring in his step, despite his leg, knowing he'd be bringing home their first proper meal since they made their escape on his bike. He stopped abruptly, his heart freezing in his chest.

There ahead of him, just below the rock he had been perched on, lay the body of the Commander. It wasn't the corpse that stopped him in his tracks; it was what had been done to it.

The throat had been ripped out and the torso fileted open, its contents gone. Blood was stomped into the leaves and dirt in a six-foot circle radiating from the corpse.

Next to the carnage, Andrew looked down at the leaf-strewn ground. On the leaves, stamped in blood, was a perfect paw print, bigger than his fist.

Wolves.

With shaking hands he quickly resupplied his magazine with another five rounds and went to collect his birds, scanning the brush and checking behind him as he went. There were three birds he downed, all flat on their backs, wings outstretched. He was too busy eying the brush to celebrate his successful hunt. He squatted, feeling for the birds; picking them up by their feet as his eyes scanned for any sign of movement.

It had most likely fed during the night. Then he remembered the howl. He went back to the top of the rock to survey the scene and get a better look at the hillside just in case anything was out and about. He spotted no movement, nothing.

Well, that explains why there's no game in the area.

An unnatural predator had migrated in and taken out what little game there was. But that meant it was probably hungry, and willing to attack anything, and he and Kaya were in danger of becoming its next source of food.

Suddenly he thought of Kaya sitting there alone, unable to run. Flashes of the gory scene below mixed with the smile on Kaya's face and fear struck him like it had never struck before. He gripped the rifle in his hand and as quickly as he could made his way up the hill. His leg screamed but he pushed the pain back; back in his mind where he put all the things that hurt, like the memory of his parents. He pushed everything back and thought only of Kaya.

CHAPTER 14
RING OF FIRE

KAYA HAD JUST PILED on the last arm full of wood for the stockpile next to the roaring fire she had built when Andrew, covered in sweat and breathing heavily, came limping into view. She went for the pistol tucked into her back pocket, thinking he was being chased by someone. But when he stopped and held up his hand while doubling over trying to catch his breath, she relaxed a little. She shifted her body, keeping her weight off her bad ankle.

"What's going on?"

"Nothing... it's okay... I... was worried... about you."

"Oh..."

Kaya was still puzzled.

"Why?"

"Wolves."

He had regained his breath somewhat, but the one word was all that was needed.

Kaya's heart stood still, fear shooting adrenaline into her veins. But then logic took over and told her to relax. Wolves weren't in this part of the country. They lived up in Canada and that Yellowstone Park, with the buffalo. This was Nevada, land of the sagebrush. Andrew was either pulling her leg or really confused. If he was kidding, it wasn't funny and she wouldn't be forgiving him anytime soon.

"Andrew, there's no wolves in Nevada."

"Tell that to the one I had a ran into back in town when I made the gas run. I've seen lots of coyotes, and this was no coyote. The Commander's body has been devoured. There's bloody paw prints on the ground the size of my fist!"

Kaya's mind was flooded with the memory of what she had done and then mixed with the gruesome picture Andrew painted. She shook her head still not able to believe it. Why now? Why them? They had guns, small guns, but no shelter, and no way to run.

"What do we do?"

She heard the panic in her own voice but didn't care. The young man before her was all she had. She knew he was strong and right now that was what she needed. She had reached the end of her resilience. She had always been able to take care of herself, and throughout life she had learned to be strong, to be independent, but she was exhausted, injured, and in a situation she had no idea how to deal with. Right now, all she wanted was someone to tell her everything was going to be alright.

Andrew, hiding the despair in his eyes, looked down at the fire, suddenly surprised at all she had done. Not only had she started the fire, but collected enough wood to keep it burning throughout the night. He thought for a few moments.

"Fire!"

"What?"

"Fire. We'll build perimeter fires and keep them burning all night. Then we will hike out of here in the morning. I read once that wolves have a territory that they stick to. We put as much distance between us and them as quickly as possible. I'll have to build you some kind of a splint for your ankle but… how did you manage to do all this?"

Kaya smiled.

"I was going nuts sitting there, so I decided to do something productive. I used a walking stick at first but it was more of a pain than it was worth. So I hopped from tree to tree, collected wood, threw it in a pile, hopped to it, and then threw it again until I got it all back here. My ankle still hurts a little but it felt good to move around again."

"But how did you start a fire?"

"I had been living out here for a while before you showed up remember? I got pretty good with the bow and drill. Jupiter taught me."

Kaya felt the tug in her chest the moment she said his name—the wound still fresh and raw.

Andrew nodded.

"We will need more wood, a lot more. It's the only defense I can think of. We'll have to make sure we collect enough to burn all night. You collect as much as you can nearby, I'll go further out. If you see anything, yell out and don't hesitate to shoot. I'll come as soon as I hear anything. Alright?"

"Alright."

Andrew smiled and walked up to her, taking her face in his hands. He stroked his thumb across her cheek and kissed her, his lips brushing hers gently at first, then more ravenous. She held him tight, relishing in his kiss and his closeness, and the comfort and safety that it exuded. They just held each other for a while, driving away each other's fears. Finally, Andrew pulled back and gazed into her eyes.

"Everything is going to be alright. We'll get through this. We'll get down off this mountain and we'll find a home for ourselves, and we can live together, normal lives. Right?"

Kaya smiled biting her lip.

"Right."

They spent the next hour collecting every piece of dry wood they could find. Kaya was exhausted. After twenty minutes she thought the pile they had made was more than enough, but when Andrew returned he said to double it.

So she trudged back out. Twice she had heard noises behind her but each time she had spun around and saw nothing.

Just nerves.

Still, she kept the pistol in one hand as she walked and continuously checked behind her. She picked up the last bits of wood she could find and tossed them on the pile in the middle of their camp.

When Andrew returned, they set about building up piles in a ring around their original fire and the stockpile of wood. The ring was about twenty feet across, and when it was done they both felt a sense of relief and safety.

Andrew and Kaya, covered in sweat and dirt, dropped to the ground next to their campfire, exhausted. With the task at hand completed, and nothing to occupy his mind, Andrew's stomach growled viciously. His mind suddenly snapped back to his morning hunt.

"The birds!"

"What?" said Kaya in a low, breathless voice. She was lying on her back, her arm draped over her eyes.

"I brought food! I killed a couple of birds just before I found the bodies. I forgot about them but I laid them next to the tree here before we started gathering wood. Come on let's have some dinner!"

Kaya had sat up quickly when he mentioned food, but then laid back down in disgust.

"No thanks," she said flatly from underneath her arm.

"What do you mean, no thanks? It's food! You haven't eaten anything for two days! If you don't, you're going to starve to death!"

"Then I'll die! But I am not eating something that had to be killed for me to stay alive."

"You're an idiot! That's how life works! Animals eat animals that eat grass! Last time I checked you can't live off of grass! That's all there is out here! We don't have the luxury of

being able to run down and buy a basket full of vegetables!
We have to live off of what the land provides."

"I'll find something else tomorrow!"

Kaya sat back, hugging her knees to her chest, tears beginning to brim.

"Fine! Suit yourself. But I've looked all over these hills.
There's nothing."

Andrew attacked the birds with his pocketknife, skinning
them out to avoid having to pluck them, and then he gutted
them. He set each finished bird on a rock next to him, and
then pulled out a tuft of grass to wipe his hands clean.

With his anger slowly subsiding, he looked at the four
birds lying there on the rock. They were small. Their fluffy
feathers had given the impression that they were nearly the
size of a small chicken, but now they looked like they had less
meat on them than a quail.

He pulled a thin limb from their wood pile and proceeded
to sharpen a point on one end. When he was satisfied with
the point he snapped off the rest of the branches. Then he
whittled off the rest of the bark, drawing it off in long strokes,
the bark curling out as it fell. Kaya watched him work next to
the fire but said nothing.

When he was finished he held the branch out over the fire,
blackening the exposed flesh of the limb. He slid each bird
onto the skewer, shoving the point out the neck holes. Propping the bobbing limb on a rock next to the fire, so that the
birds hung out over the flames at an upward angle, he then
placed a large rock at the base of the limb to hold it in place.

The fire crackled and sizzled as fat began to drip down.
Soon the savory scent of meat was in the air and Andrew's
mouth was salivating well before the meat was done, but he
forced himself to wait. His stomach aching in anticipation.

Andrew knew the smell of the birds and their entrails
would probably attract unwanted visitors, but he figured the
scent of him and Kaya would be enough to draw the wolves

anyway. Better to eat and have the energy to hike out in the morning.

He sliced into the lowest bird, the one closest to the flames. Its outside was beginning to blacken and when he sliced into it, it looked done, but in the firelight it was difficult to tell if the juices were clear or if there was still blood in the tough meat. He decided it was close enough and cut off a small piece, blowing on it until his fingers could take the heat no more and tossed it into his mouth. It burned going down but it was good. The meat was gamey and a little tough and stringy, but to him it tasted like Thanksgiving turkey.

Andrew cut small chunks of the birds off and set the still sizzling pieces on a flat rock next to him, blowing on his finger between each piece. He broke down two of the birds into pieces and left the other one to cook longer. He began pecking at pieces on the rock, grabbing, blowing, and then nibbling the tiny bits of meat off the bone. His stomach caused his heart to race, telling him to eat more and eat faster. It was in starvation mode.

He looked to Kaya. She was still sitting, watching him silently. He thought he saw her shaking too, but he couldn't be sure in the flickering light.

"Kaya, please eat. We need our strength tomorrow. If we're going to make it out of here you're going to need something. I need you with me, Kaya. I..." He stopped, unable to finish, afraid of looking stupid. Afraid of what she might say. He turned back to the fire, staring at the dancing embers.

"What?" Her voice cracked from her silence, but he said nothing and just stared at the fire.

Kaya crawled over and sat next to him, hooking her arm through his. He turned and their eyes met and she gave a hint of a smile. She sat for a while but she reluctantly reached for a chunk of meat. She turned it over, examining it. Finally, she took a deep breath, closed her eyes, and took a small bite. She chewed slowly, cautiously.

"Oh my god. It's good. It's actually, really good," she said taking another bite.

They ate until there was not a scrap left and then Andrew cut up the last bird. Andrew smiled and gave her a peck on the cheek. Her mouth widened into a silly grin and when she could hold it no longer, started to giggle hysterically. Andrew laughed too. All he could think was how beautiful she was, laughing, her eyes glistening, and the light from the flames dancing on her face in the fading evening light.

She saw him staring at her and slowly her giggling began to subside. She felt his eyes on her and knew what he was thinking, what he wanted. With their arms still hooked, she leaned in and kissed him passionately. It was a long kiss full of fire. She untangled her arm from his and placed her hand on his chest pushing him back to the ground. She followed him down, their lips never parting. His arms encircled her, his hands resting on her back just below the hem of her shirt. He slid his hands beneath the material and slowly moved them up her back. Suddenly he stopped.

"Did you hear that?" he whispered breathlessly.

"No. What?"

"I don't... I thought I heard something."

A twig snapped to his left somewhere out in the darkness, followed by a low rumbling growl.

"Something's out there... the fires!"

Andrew and Kaya scrambled to get up from their bed of twigs and pine needles. They frantically pulled chunks of wood from the fire, tossing them to each pile of wood spraying sparks into the air. They worked in a fierce frenzy; fear driving them like a slave-master's whip. The fires lit and were soon roaring all around them.

Andrew snatched up his rifle and aimed into the darkness turning 360 degrees, looking for any sign. He stopped, he was watching the embers rise from the flames up into the blackness of the night, but two had caught his eye. They weren't rising and the color was wrong. They were eyes, staring back at him. Andrew didn't hesitate; he fired a round between the two floating eyes. When he looked again they were gone, but he couldn't be sure he had hit anything. A moment later a loud howl sent shivers up their backs. They both raised their guns in the direction of the bone-chilling sound, and waited. A silence settled over the camp, and Andrew felt like time was standing still.

Suddenly the wind howled through the camp, hurling smoke and sparks at Kaya and Andrew, burning their eyes and filling their lungs. They huddled together, coughing, rubbing at their tearing eyes, listening as best they could; their guns pointing into the darkness, waiting. They could feel it, the breath of death circling them, trying to find the weakness in their defenses, the chink in their armor. All they could do was wait.

———

They took turns taking watch while the other attempted to sleep. They kept the fires fed but their stockpile dwindled. They had no idea what time it was, or how long until dawn would come. Andrew sat back against the tree and tried to close his stinging eyes and rest, but his mind was a spinning jumble of thoughts. He just wanted to get Kaya and himself back to safety, to someplace to call home. He pictured a home, a farm, animals, a garden, and Kaya. He saw her picking flowers, happy, and he held the image in his mind, willing it to come to be.

"Ahhh!" screamed Kaya.

Andrew shot up, spinning in a circle, looking for the wolf, but there was just Kaya. She was standing next to the inner-most fire, doubled over, her arms wrapped around her middle.

"What's wrong?"

"It's... my stomach. The meat... has to be."

She spoke through gritted teeth in obvious pain.

"I haven't had it... in so long. My stomach can't handle it... anymore."

"Here, sit down."

Andrew guided her to the tree and she sat still holding her stomach. Andrew found the holster, still full of water and gave it to her.

"Have some water."

She managed to get down a sip, but nearly dropped it shoving it back to him.

"I can't, it hurts too much."

"I know but you have to try."

He handed it back but she didn't take it. She stayed doubled over, clutching her stomach. He gave in and placed it against a rock next to the fire. As his hand left the holster, he got an idea. He repositioned the rock so that it was partially in the fire, and placed the holster right next to the coals. Then he stripped off a handful of pine needles from the tree above and dumped them into the water.

About five minutes passed and finally he could see steam rising from the water. The outside started to char and smoke. Kaya had recovered some but he could tell she was still in pain. Andrew picked up the holster, testing it to see if it was too hot to hold. It wasn't bad so he held it out to Kaya.

"Here, try to get some of this down. The hot water will help just try not to drink the pine needles. My mom taught me that pine needle tea is good for the stomach."

He felt a pang in his chest at the thought of his mother and wondered if it would always be that way.

Kaya took the tea and held it close to her for a moment, staring at it and then took a sip and then another. She let her hands drop to her legs, still holding the hot liquid. She tilted her head back against the tree and closed her eyes. After a few minutes, Andrew almost thought that in the firelight he could see color returning to her face.

"It's easing up a bit," she said quietly, taking another small sip.

"Good."

Andrew smiled and breathed a sigh of relief.

"What else did your mom teach you?" asked Kaya, her eyes still closed.

Andrew was silent for a time before he answered, thinking back and remembering. He laughed a little then.

"She taught me to sew. My Grandma always had old soft, heavy quilts. They were so comfy. Nothing could keep you warmer. So I wanted my own quilt and Mom taught me how to sew it. It had deer and trees and buffalo printed on the material. I was pretty proud of it. I even bragged about it to all my buddies at school. I got made fun of for a month. But that's school right? Tease before somebody teases you. Hurt before someone else hurts you."

He sighed.

"Well, it doesn't matter now. I was still proud of that quilt. Wish I had it now. Kaya?"

She was breathing deeply, her head back against the tree, snoring softly. Andrew pulled the rest of her pine needle tea from her limp fingers and set it aside and gently lifted her, moving her away from the tree, laying her down next to the fire. He brushed her hair out her face and pulled a leaf from her hair. He saw a crack of a smile form on her lips. He leaned over, kissing the little spot where her cheek and her lips met.

Andrew rose and fed the fires, staring into the flames, once again holding the happy vision of Kaya in his mind. He thought that if he wanted it bad enough and held the picture in his mind clearly enough, then the desert would grant his wish.

Late into the night, Andrew sat down next to the sleeping form of Kaya. He was done in. His eyes, watering from the smoke, felt the heavy weight of his eyelids like a ton of bricks pushing him downward towards the soft, warm, leaf-covered earth.

I'll just rest my eyes for a few seconds, just a few...

He drifted off to sleep almost instantly.

————

Kaya crept slowly up to the creature, careful not to make a noise. She held the pistol in her hand. Its back was to her, she needed to get as close as possible. Her heart raced and her palm was slick with sweat against the grip of the gun. A twig snapped beneath her foot and she froze. She held her breath, waiting for the beast to turn and charge, but it didn't. She moved a step and then another, still the animal didn't stir. She was close enough now; she lifted the pistol and aimed it at the back of its head.

Suddenly it turned around and instead of the beast it was the Commander. She fired, hitting him in the head, but he kept coming. She kept firing, but each round was quieter and quieter, like duds that barely left a mark on his forehead. He reached for her and shoved her down. His hand went to her throat squeezing the life from her body, the other hand wielding long sharp claws slashed into her stomach. He was saying something but she could barely hear him. She tried to tell him she couldn't hear him but her voice was lost. Finally as the blood oozed from her abdomen, he screamed at her, *'HE'S WATCHING YOU!'*.

Kaya's eyes snapped open, her heart was pounding and her head ached. She looked around. The fires were now a circle of glowing coal, with smoke slowly rising from the ashes. It was near dawn, the sky was gray and it was cold. She could smell the icy dew and feel it on her face. Andrew was next to her, his back to her, sound asleep. Her eyes panned across the fire line and the trees beyond; they stopped on a hazy area of trees in front of her. Something had caught her eye. She couldn't tell what it was but something wasn't right with the clump of trees in front of her. She peered harder, trying to focus through the rising waves of heat. A small breeze came up blowing at the smoke and for a second her vision cleared and she saw it; big and gray with cold black eyes staring right back at her.

Kaya squeezed Andrew's arm hard, willing him to wake up without a sound. The pistol was inside her coat. She slipped her hand in without taking her eyes off the wolf. Her fingers wrapped around the grip, bringing it slowly to her lap. The creature didn't move. She shook his arm roughly. Finally he stirred.

"What... hmm?"

"Look," she hissed, still without taking her eyes from the staring beast.

Andrew blinked, rubbing the sleep from his eyes. He peered in the direction she indicated.

"Kaya, I don't..."

Then he saw it, and he felt the blood drain from his face. He looked to his left and snatched up his rifle. He shoved himself to his feet, but they were unsteady and his hamstring was sore and tight. He braced himself back against the tree and raised the small rifle, but as he took aim, the wolf disappeared. He blinked hard a couple of times, thinking he just wasn't focusing. Kaya quickly got to her feet.

"Where did it go?" she whispered.

"I don't know."

Andrew spun in a slow circle, forcing his still sleep-filled eyes to focus in the low light, waiting for any sign of movement, waiting for the wolf to charge from the trees. His peripherals picked up a mound of gray fur to his left and he quickly trained his sights on it and pulled the trigger. But nothing happened; the safety was still on. He slid his finger back and popped the little button sideways, disengaging the safety. Andrew's finger rested back on the smooth trigger, but he didn't pull it, he watched, something wasn't right. He could see gray fur, he was sure; but it was low to the ground and not moving. He couldn't see the head either; it had to be just sitting there.

Andrew stepped up to the edge of the coals and peered over them, trying to make sense of what he was seeing. Was it just lying there watching him? He rested his cheek back on the smooth wood stock of the rifle and raised the sights between his eye and the wolf again.

He was confused; he felt a strange pang of guilt, a hesitance, to shoot an animal just sitting there. Finally his brain figured out what his eyes were telling him. He focused and could see its head, lying flat on the ground, tilted strangely. It was dead. It was the wolf from last night and he had killed it.

Andrew stepped over the fire and looked around, making sure the other one wasn't waiting for him, but he saw nothing. He walked cautiously up to the mass of soft-looking fur rippling in the morning breeze. He kept his rifle pointed at it, half expecting the beast to come back to life and leap for him. But the body of the wolf never moved even when he pushed on it with the tip of his barrel.

Kaya was behind him, watching with one eye and scanning the brush with the other, her pistol at the ready. Still rattled from her dream and not certain that this wasn't still part of it, she stayed silent, rifling through her thoughts, attempting to separate hallucination from reality. It was all a dream now; stuck in the mountains with a boy, chased by wolves, hunted by evil men, one of which she killed, her grandfather executed, her parents dead, taken by an ungodly virus. None of it seemed real anymore. She was in a dream, a nightmare, and she yearned to wake up.

Andrew knelt to examine the wolf, lifting its head. There was one small hole on the left side of the forehead at the top of a dark trickle of dried blood, matting the soft gray fur where it pooled at its neck.

"We could use the fur, but I won't have to time to clean it properly, plus I don't think I want the scent of it with us. The other one will be able to track us easy enough as it is. I think we should just get going."

"Do you think there's more than one still out there?"

"I don't know. Lee told me that lone males will go out on their own, after getting kicked out of the pack. These could be just two males that were running together. That would mean that we would only have one more to deal with, but it also means he doesn't have a territory to stick to and we killed its only friend."

"Flipping fantastic. We're living in nightmare."

"How are you feeling?"

"Better."

"Think your ankle is ready for a hike? I'll find some good straight sticks to make a splint for you."

Kaya nodded, knowing she didn't have much of a choice.

"Alright, let's get the hell out of here."

CHAPTER 15
UNEXPECTED GUESTS

THEY HAD TRAVELED for two days and seen no sign of the wolf. Each night they recreated their protective ring of fire. Running had become their lives, their world, all that mattered. Their sole focus was pushing forward and finding their next source of water and food.

They reached the north end of the mountain range, where it dropped steeply to the valley floor. To the northwest started another range of mountains that looked much taller than the ones they had just left, already with traces of snow along the ridges. Across the open valley, at least fifteen miles to the east was another range of smaller hills.

The valley was flat as far as they could tell, covered in a smooth carpet of grayish-green sagebrush. But Andrew knew the valleys of the desert could be deceptive. Canyons, river beds, valleys within valleys, all hidden within the sage.

Andrew and Kaya had spotted a thin winding line in the sagebrush dividing the valley that they hoped was a riverbed. They made their way down through the dense brush, and by midday had reached the valley floor. They trudged along making their way in the general direction of the river bed, no longer able to see it from their vantage point. The sagebrush was nearly six feet tall here, practically trees; trees that blocked the way, pulling at their hair, grabbing at loose clothing, and scratching any exposed skin with their multitude of spindly branches. Twice Andrew had pushed through only to release the branches he was battling right as Kaya was coming through, whipping her in the face.

"Alright! That's it. I'm going in front. I'm tired of getting whipped in the face by those stupid things!"

"Oh, shoot, I'm sorry. Did I get you again? You gotta not follow so close."

Kaya said nothing and pushed past him, diving into the brush ahead. Andrew let out a sigh and followed after her. He pushed past a big brush and caught just a glimpse of Kaya as she fought ahead. He struggled to keep up, but she was practically sprinting ahead.

"I guess your ankle is feeling better?" he yelled but was answered with silence as Kaya disappeared once again.

No, not like we should stick together or anything. Whatever. She's got a gun, and good luck to anything out here brave enough to take her on. Maybe a really feisty badger. I hope not, for the badger's sake.

Andrew laughed to himself, until suddenly he heard her scream, followed by a splash.

"Kaya?!"

He ran, pushing at the brush, ducking and diving through. Suddenly the brush opened up to nothingness. Instinctively, he dropped to his butt and his feet slid to a stop at the edge of the cliff. He got up and peered over the edge, dreading what he was about to see. There ten feet below him was the river, although anywhere other than Nevada, it would be called a creek.

Crawling over the rocky beach on the far side was Kaya, on all fours, soaking wet, looking very much like a cat that got too close to the pool. Andrew, to his horror, felt an urge of laughter swelling up that was threatening to pour out of him at the sad sight.

"Ka... Kaya!"

He bit his lip.

"Are you okay?"

He nearly lost his voice, holding back his amusement.

"No! I'm not okay! I'm cold and I'm wet and it's not funny!"

Andrew struggled to regain his composure; he knew he wasn't earning any brownie points. He looked up and down the river. It was typical of desert water ways he had seen, a series of consecutive s-turns, slowly eating away at the soft desert dirt.

"How deep is it right here?"

Kaya just glared.

"Oh come on, I'm sorry. I know you could have gotten hurt. I shouldn't have laughed. Okay?"

Kaya sat glaring at him long enough to let him know this wouldn't be the end of it.

"It's deep. Five or six feet. Lucky too. If it had been any shallower I probably would have shattered my ankle! Then you'd really be laughing, having to carry me the rest of the way!"

"I think I'd take the 'horse with a broken leg' approach," he mumbled to himself.

"What was that?"

Pretending not to hear her, he slid down the bank and quickly stripped down to his underwear. He dropped his gun atop the pile of clothes and leaped into the air. Before the splash of water had even landed on the rocks, he was back up gasping for the air that the icy water had stolen from his lungs.

"What are you doing?"

"Holy shit it's cold!"

Andrew scrambled up the slippery rocks and stood before

Kaya. She was huddled in a ball, still in her wet clothes, shivering.

"Come on, strip. You're not going to get warm that way and you're definitely not going to get clean after just one dip. Come on, you need to drink some too."

"You want me to get naked?"

Andrew grinned.

He held out his goosebump-riddled arm to her. Kaya stood and reluctantly peeled off her soggy clothes, stripping down to her panties. Feeling exposed, she wrapped her arms around her body covering herself. Standing there nearly naked and shivering was anything but romantic. Hesitantly she took his outstretched hand and allowed herself to be led back to the chilly waters. He led her in until the water reached their calves. The shock felt invigorating to Andrew; Kaya on the other hand had wrapped herself back up in her arms and was chattering her teeth. Andrew took her in his arms and began rubbing her back and arms vigorously.

"Does that help?"

She nodded, with a stiff mechanical movement. He managed to coax her further so that the water was up to their thighs. Despite the cold, Andrew struggled to keep his eyes off her bare skin.

"Getting used to it?"

"A little."

The chattering slowed.

"Okay, because here comes the worst part." He said as he guided them into the deepest part, the water rushing well above their torsos.

They both gasped, holding their breath, until their bodies had slowly adjusted to the cold. They took turns dunking their heads beneath the frigid water, hurriedly scrubbing with fingernails at the grit and grime that had taken up residence on their bodies.

They staggered back to the warmth of the rocks, stumbling on cold-numbed feet. As they sat down, the warmth of the rocks on their bare skin sent shivers up their spines, but it wasn't enough. A slight breeze kept any warmth that might be radiating from the sun pushed away. Andrew scrambled up and began searching for sticks to burn. Soon he had an armful and set about building a fire. Over the past few days Kaya had been teaching him how to start a fire with a bow and drill. She was happy to have been able to teach him something for a change.

His cold hands fumbled blindly, trying to remove one of Kaya's shoelaces; his was still across the river. Finally, it pulled free and he tied it to both ends of his bow, bending it as he did so, so that the string would be tight. He wrapped the lace around a stick he had found for his drill and used a dished rock as a block to hold his drill in place. The drill whined as he began pushing and pulling on the bow, slowly at first to allow the drill to bed itself into the piece below. When he was confident it wouldn't slip, he increased his speed, turning the bow and drill to a blur.

The cold was getting to him. His muscles wanted to retract and send blood to warm his vital organs. A chill ran up his back and he started to shiver. A spark of hope emerged as smoke began to rise from the base of his drill. Excitedly he picked up the pace, but as he did so, the base slipped out sending his tinder and his small ember flying.

"Damn it!"

He cursed himself as he wrapped his tingling arms around himself, warming his hands under his armpits.

"You got too excited. Slow and steady wins the race, remember?"

Kaya had curled up into a ball once again, the sun teasing her skin with occasional touches of warmth.

Andrew collected his bits of wood, re-situated his tinder, and started again. It felt like an eternity had passed when the smoke finally started to rise again. Andrew held his pace, and Kaya crawled over and began blowing on the ember.

"Okay, that's good," said Kaya.

Andrew stopped and carefully removed the drill, making sure not to disturb the glowing ember. Kaya tilted the base, rolling the ember onto the nest of tinder and continued to blow. Smoke poured from the pile as the tiny ember struggled to take hold. Kaya turned her head each time to take a breath of fresh air, then turned back to continue blowing. Finally, the smoking tinder erupted in flames. Andrew had been ready and began feeding small twigs and dry grass to the flames.

Before long they had a roaring fire, each of them sitting as close as possible to the flames without burning themselves. Andrew heated water with the holster, saturating it first, and then propping it against a rock near the flames. When it started to steam he handed it to Kaya. She shuddered, wrapping her hands around the warmed, charred leather and slowly sipped. She let out a sigh of near ecstasy as the warm liquid flowed down her throat.

Andrew held his hands near the flames, rubbing warmth back into them. He glanced across the water at his pile of clothes and rifle. He sighed, shaking his head. He stood, steeling himself for one more plunge.

After retrieving his things he thoroughly washed his and her clothes in the water, whipping them against rocks. Satisfied, he draped the clothes over the branches of the sagebrush to dry in the slight breeze.

When he was finished he rejoined Kaya. Together they sat on a small patch of sand in front of the fire, holding hands, watching the sun sink closer to the horizon. They reveled in the feeling of the warm sand beneath their feet while soaking up the last of the sun.

Neither had said anything for quite a while, each in their trance as the sun painted the sky with pinks, purples, and reds so vivid, one would swear it was a painting. When the shadow of twilight reached them and the sun disappeared below the mountains, they stirred.

"So what's for dinner sweetie?" said Andrew.

"Eggplant and tofu casserole, with a side of hummus," Kaya replied matter-of-factly.

Andrew pretended to gag and was about to reply with a comeback when he froze. He could hear something moving through the brush.

He leaped to his feet, snatching up his rifle. Kaya reached for her clothes and pistol, thumbing down the safety. It was coming slowly, making its way through the brush, and then it stopped.

They held their breath, waiting.

"Hello to camp."

They glanced at each other, shock on their faces.

"Anyone there? I come in peace!"

"Come slowly into the light, we're armed," said Andrew.

Slowly a figure emerged, pushing past a large sage-brush. It was a young man. Looked to be eighteen, twenty maybe, Andrew guessed. He was dressed like a cowboy; boots, jeans, buttoned shirt, but no hat. He had a belt filled with bullets that shined in the firelight and on his hip Andrew could see the curved wooden handle of a six-shooter. Andrew felt like they had stepped into the Old West.

"I saw the smoke from your fire a few hours ago, and I figured I'd..."

The man stopped, cocking his head, realizing that Kaya and Andrew were mostly naked. Kaya quickly covered herself.

"I didn't mean to... if I interrupted something I can come back later," he said, sounding a bit embarrassed.

"That won't be necessary. You were saying?" said Andrew still not lowering his guard.

"Right. Like I was saying... I saw your fire and figured I'd come and investigate... I uh... haven't seen another person around here in quite a while."

Obviously uncomfortable, the man tried to keep eye contact with Andrew, but his eyes continuously dodged from him to Kaya, then quickly to the ground.

"You live alone out here?" asked Andrew.

"About ten miles up the valley at my family's ranch. I was hunting when I spotted your smoke. I wasn't sure what to expect, but I haven't seen anyone in so long I had to come."

"What about your family? Where are they?" Kaya spoke up for the first time.

"About a year ago mom and dad loaded up with all the gas we had and drove down to Reno to look for my sister. She was going to school down there and we hadn't heard anything from her since everything started to go bad. That was the last time I talked to them."

His eyes cast down and he went quiet. Andrew and Kaya did the same, both thinking about their own parents.

Finally Andrew spoke up.

"I suppose you're telling the truth, but we'd be a whole lot more comfortable if you dropped your gun. We have been shot at enough here lately, that we prefer to err on the side of caution."

"I don't blame you. I'll make you a deal--I'll drop mine if you drop yours."

Andrew squatted down and laid his rifle out in front of him. As he did so, the man unlatched his belt buckle and lowered his belt to the ground taking a step forward. He took another step and held out his hand.

"I'm Avery by the way."

Andrew stood and took his hand.

"I'm Andrew, and this is Kaya."

"Pleasure to meet you both. So what brings you all the way out here?"

"Well, we... my aunt and uncle have a ranch out here..."

Kaya interrupted.

"If you'll excuse me, *I* am going to get some clothes on."

She backed into the darkness clutching her pile of clothes. Andrew continued.

"I'm from Alturas, just over the California border, west of Cedarville."

Avery nodded.

"Sure, I know Alturas."

"We had a farm on the edge of town. A group of soldiers came in and killed everyone, including my parents." He paused, choking back tears. "It looked like they were burning the whole town. I got away, barely. I managed to make it over the state line on my motorcycle, but the men followed me."

"Damn shame about your folks. Sorry," said Avery.

Andrew nodded in appreciation and continued.

"There was a man, the Commander, who for whatever reason, was hell-bent on catching me. I made it to a trapper's cabin but they caught up with me there. They tortured me, cut off my finger, then they stuck a knife between my ribs."

He held up his hand, displaying the nub where his pinky had been.

"I swear," said Avery, shaking his head.

"Luckily Lee, the trapper, showed up about then and killed two of the men, but the Commander got away. Lee nursed me back to health. It was a few weeks before I could even move much. He was a good man. He saved my life."

"Was?" asked Avery.

"I would imagine he's dead now, but I don't know. After I left him I found Kaya and her grandfather. That's where the Commander found me again. The last time he saw me I was in a pool of my own blood. He had to of gone back to Lee's to even know I was still alive. I guess he thought he had a score to settle."

Andrew glanced up as Kaya emerged from the shadows,

fully clothed and pulling her hair back. He stared at her in the firelight, longer than he meant to.

"Are you planning to put some clothes on or just stand there half naked all night?" said Kaya.

The moment was gone. Andrew glanced down at himself, having almost forgotten that he was still in just his underwear.

"Yeah, I guess I should get some clothes on," said Andrew, realizing he was starting to shiver from the cold.

Avery laughed.

"Please, I'll bet you're half freezing."

"It is a little chilly. Have a seat by the fire, Avery."

"Much obliged," said Avery moving over to warm his hands by the fire.

Andrew pulled his pants and shirt from the limbs of the sagebrush and whipped them in the air a few times. He slid on his pants; they were stiff and despite their appearance, they at least felt clean. More importantly, they were dry.

"Well it sounds like you've had quite an adventure. What have y'all been eating? This country has gotten pretty scarce ever since those goddamn wolves showed up."

"Not much," said Kaya.

"We had some bird, some kind of blackbird I guess, two... maybe three days ago." Said Andrew

"What? Shit, you guys must be starving! I'll be right back."

Andrew glanced at Kaya and raised his eyebrows. He was pulling on his shirt when Avery appeared again this time with a horse in tow.

"Now it may not be a steak dinner but on an empty stomach, it's gonna taste like it."

Avery dove into his saddle bags and emerged with two cans, and tucking those beneath his arm, quickly returned for two more. He turned and set the four cans down beside the fire, then headed for the other side of his horse.

"Oh I'm sorry. How rude of me. Everyone this is Bonnie."

"Awe. Can I pet her?" cooed Kaya.

Kaya was beside herself with what Andrew could only describe as actual giddiness.

"Sure. Scratch her butt and she'll be your best friend! She's a bit of a sellout that way."

Avery had dove into the saddlebag on the opposite side, searching frantically for something.

"Awe, she's so pretty."

She stroked the mare's nose and then scratched her neck.

"Found it."

Avery strode around Bonnie and Kaya carrying a small pot and a can opener. He sat down next to Andrew by the fire and began working at the cans.

"Thank you for sharing your food, Avery. We ate a couple of stringy black birds a couple days," said Andrew.

"Don't mention it. It's just beans but after all you been through, it's the least I can do."

Avery quickly had all four cans open and dumped their contents into the pot. He nestled the pot into the coals and sat back, staring at the fire. Kaya had moved on to untangling Bonnie's mane, lost to the world. Finally, Andrew broke the silence.

"So you've seen the wolves?"

"Yessir, just two of them out here as far as I know. Males I'm guessing. No sign of pups. I've seen them a few times when I was out hunting, one's dark gray and one's light. I stumbled onto one of their kills one time. Luckily I was on horseback or they probably would have tried to take me. Each time I see them they disappear before I can get a shot off though. Sneaky bastards."

"Well they visited us a few days ago. I managed to kill the lighter one. The other one is still out there, but I think I might have wounded it back when I was in that little town to the south."

"Wow! Killed one of the brutes, eh? You guys might be handy to have around."

"It was a lucky shot in the dark," admitted Andrew.

"But it's the light one you killed? That's the smaller one. That's not good. I would imagine the darker one is on your tail then."

"I don't think so. We have been watching our trail and haven't seen any sign of him since that night."

Andrew's eyes were drawn to the steaming pot near the fire as the savory aroma of beans hit his nose. His stomach growled and ached with anticipation.

"Hmm, well don't rule it out, he's still out there. Wolves are pack creatures, like families and they aren't forgiving. Now then, I think the beans are hot."

Avery pulled the pot out of the coals, giving it a stir, and set it on a rock next to him. He then began spooning the steaming beans back into three of the cans.

"Give me a minute," he said passing one of the full cans to Andrew.

Taking one of the aluminum can lids, Avery pressed it against a rock with his thumb, folding it like a taco shell. Then he folded up one of the ends, forming a primitive spoon, and handed it to Andrew.

"Sorry, I don't have more utensils. I've only got one spoon. So you get a primitive one. Careful you don't cut your lip on it."

He fashioned one more of these spoons and set it to the side for himself and then deposited the real spoon into the third can for Kaya.

Andrew examined the homemade utensil and then took a great scoop of his beans, nodding with approval.

"That's pretty nifty," he said his mouth with his sleeve. "You're a pro at this, aren't you? Oh, these are good. Oh, Kaya. Kaya check this out… Kaya, you going to eat?"

"Huh? What... oh yes. I'm starving!"

She quickly returned to the fire and took a seat between Avery and Andrew, accepting the piping hot can that was offered to her.

"Nah I'm no pro, I just spend a lot of time out under the stars eating from a campfire. Seems to suit me," said Avery, staring up into the sky. "Being home just reminds me of what I've lost. Out here I can find some peace."

Kaya and Andrew's eyes followed his gaze upward.

"I know what you mean, but I like a bed and a shower. God, how long has it been since I have had a shower?" Kaya sighed in dismay.

"Awhile," said Andrew.

Kaya jabbed him in the ribs with her elbow and he burst out laughing.

"I haven't heard any complaints."

"Don't get me wrong I do enjoy being able to go home, sleep in my warm bed, and it's pretty hard to beat a good hot shower. I just like spending my time out here, like the old days, you know?"

"Wait, wait, wait... did you say *hot* shower? You have power?" asked Kaya nearly dropping her can of beans.

"Well we do have a couple of solar panels but the hot water heater would soak up too much juice. No, I have a couple of solar showers. You fill them up and then hang them in the sun to heat, works pretty nice. You're both welcome to try them out tomorrow."

"Oh thank you, thank you, thank you!"

Kaya set down her can and jumped at Avery hugging him around the neck.

Andrew felt a slight pang of jealousy when she hugged Avery, but it passed. In truth, he was as thrilled as she was and he could have hugged the man as well.

"Really, it's no problem. I'd be glad to have some house guests. You guys are welcome to stay until you get your strength back."

A wave of relief swept over Andrew at the prospect of sleeping in a house, safe, eating warm food, and getting to take a shower. Looking back he couldn't believe what they had grown accustomed to.

"We appreciate it, Avery. It's been a long time since we have seen any kind of normal. If you know what I mean."

"I understand, really no big deal."

Kaya stopped eating suddenly and clutched her stomach.

"Kaya, are you okay?" asked Andrew.

"What's in the beans?" she asked through gritted teeth.

Avery examined the cans.

"Um, well, let's see... none have hit their expiration date yet. I already checked. Close but should still be safe. There's one can of garbanzo beans, two of black beans, and... chili with burger. "

Kaya froze.

"Burger?" she repeated.

"Yup. That's what it says, burger might be stretching it. It's canned chili. I have a feeling they don't exactly use grade A meat."

"Oh, shit," said Andrew. "She's vegan... or vegetarian. She gets bad stomach aches whenever she has meat."

"Ah Shit. I'm sorry. I didn't know."

"It's alright it'll pass. The same thing happened with the bird meat."

Andrew jumped up and went to fill the holster at the stream. It was dried out, and beginning to crack and leak, but after a moment the dry leather soaked up the water and sealed itself once again. Andrew brought it back to the fire and set it to heat. Avery watched intently.

"What are you doing?"

"Making her some tea... er, hot water. It helped last time," said Andrew.

"Oh. In that thing? I've got a cup if you like…"

Avery jumped to his feet.

"I have tea bags too. Mint tea to be exact, always settles my stomach. Here I'll get one."

Avery dove once again into his saddle bags, pushing things back and forth, clanging and rattling. Andrew scooted next to Kaya and put his arm around her, rubbing her back. Kaya dropped her head to his shoulder clutching her stomach still, her eyes closed tight.

"I was so hungry I didn't think to ask."

"You were distracted by the pretty pony," said Andrew.

"I like her," she whispered.

"Damn, come on don't tell me I'm all out… bingo! I knew I had a few left."

He returned to the fire, holding up a small tea bag and a blue enameled cup.

"Thanks, Avery. I think that'll help."

Andrew leaned forward, carefully picking up the steaming holster and poured it into the cup. He took the tea bag and dipped it into the water, dunking it a few times before letting it sink to the bottom. He held it up close to Kaya's mouth.

"Do you feel like you can drink a little?"

She nodded, taking the cup in her hands, and then lifted her head from his shoulder, sipping the hot liquid. She let out a long breath and returned to the comfort of his shoulder. She lowered the cup and held it in her lap.

"Thank you, that's really good," said Kaya softly.

"I'm sorry I should have said something," said Avery looking worried.

"It's alright you didn't know. We hadn't eaten anything for days and when finally I killed those birds I made her eat some. It was bad then."

Avery nodded silently, staring into the fire. He got up suddenly and rummaged through his saddlebags once more, pulling out another can.

"Here's a can of peaches. That was the last of my beans.

Wished I wouldn't have mixed them. But at least you can get something in your stomach."

"Thank you, Avery. That sounds good," said Kaya with her eyes closed and head still on Andrews shoulder.

Avery removed the lid and brought the canned peaches handing them to Andrew. He took it and held it in his lap, while he licked Kaya's spoon clean, and waited until Kaya was ready. Avery turned back to his horse.

"I'm sorry Bonnie. I left you standing there with your saddle on. Had that stupid thing on most of the day haven't you? Let's get you ready for bed. Well, that is if you all don't mind me sharing your camp?"

"Of course not, we're already in your debt," said Andrew.

"Forget it. It's well worth it having some company," said Avery.

He scratched Bonnie's head and then began loosening the leather straps, then in one quick motion slipped the saddle off her back and set it over next to the fire where he had been sitting. He then returned with a multicolored blanket that had been under the saddle and began rubbing down her back where the saddle had been. When he was done, he laid the blanket out over the top of the saddle and then removed the reins and bridle.

Bonnie licked her lips and stretched her jaw, her mouth free of the metal bit. She immediately bent down to chew on a tuft of grass growing between the rocks. Avery stretched out on the ground settling back into the dip of his saddle.

Kaya stirred and held the tea up to her lips once again, this time she took a larger sip and then another.

"Feeling better?" he asked.

"Yeah, a little. I think I'll try some peaches."

"You never did tell me what happened with the man that was after you, the Captain?"

"The Commander," said Andrew softly.

"Right, the Commander. So did he get away?"

Andrew felt Kaya nod ever so slightly as if giving him permission to tell him. Andrew kissed her on the head and then took a long deep breath and launched into the story of the execution of her grandfather and how Kaya killed the Commander. Avery listened with rapt attention, occasionally asking questions.

It was late into the night when the conversation died down between Andrew and Avery. Kaya had begun to snore softly on Andrew's shoulder and he decided it was time for him to sleep as well. Rolling up his jacket for a pillow, he laid back slowly taking Kaya with him.

Avery got up, tossed a few more branches on the fire, and then settled in for the night against his saddle, draping his jacket over himself and working his shoulders down onto the seat. The night was calm and peaceful, for the moment.

CHAPTER 16
REVENGE COMES IN THE NIGHT

ANDREW'S EYES SNAPPED OPEN. He listened carefully but heard nothing. It was still dark, yet he was wide awake, something had stirred him. Reaching out he felt the smooth cold grain of his rifle stock. Then he heard, or felt rather, a soft thud, then two more. A pause and then it started again. He looked around, but it was too dark to see. He gently pulled out from underneath Kaya's sleeping form, sliding his jacket beneath her head before he removed his arm. He hefted his gun and waited. There it was again.

Thud, thud, thud, pause, thud, thud.

Then he heard a snort and realized it was Avery's horse, Bonnie. She was pawing at the ground with her large hooves. She whinnied softly. Andrew didn't know a thing about horses but there was no doubt in his mind that something was wrong. He listened but heard nothing except Bonnie's side to side pacing and then more pawing. She whinnied again, this time louder. Instantly Avery sprang up from his bed, rising with his pistol.

"Avery, something's wrong," hissed Andrew.

Avery walked slowly over to Bonnie, listening intently.

With one hand he scratched her neck and head trying to calm her.

"Shh. What's the matter? You're alright girl. Take it easy."

He whispered into her ear and stroked her neck but she just seemed to become more agitated. Suddenly her nostrils flared, her ears pinned back and her eyes went wide. She breathed in heavily and began backing up. Avery took hold of her halter in an attempt to keep her from bolting.

"Something's out there. You better wake Kaya," Avery whispered.

Andrew knelt still keeping his gun up and shook Kaya gently.

"Kaya, Kaya wake up. Something is coming. I need you to put some more wood on the fire."

Kaya sat up quickly looking around; trying to make sure she wasn't dreaming. Then quickly, she got up and tossed in a few branches that were near the fire. They waited. Nothing could be heard except Bonnie's deep snorting and the now popping of the fire. Suddenly Bonnie's head turned, looking back behind her and instantly she spun around.

"Shit," hissed Avery, narrowly avoiding being knocked over. "Kaya add the rest of the wood, I think this is your wolf."

Kaya added what was left on the pile and the flames rose, popping and dancing nearly three feet high.

"Kaya, there is a rifle in a scabbard on my saddle. Would you bring it to me please?" said Avery softly.

Kaya did what he asked and brought him the rifle; its yellow brass shimmered in the light.

"Here take this," he said trading the pistol to her for the rifle.

He held the rifle in one hand and Bonnie's halter in the other. He looked up at Bonnie and his shoulders seemed to droop in the firelight. With a snap of his thumb, he released the buckle on her halter. Avery clicked his tongue twice and she immediately spun and galloped away in the opposite direction.

"What are you doing? How will you get her back?" Kaya's voice cracked.

"She'll head back to the ranch, I hope. But if that wolf comes running in here I won't be able to control her and I won't be able to shoot. She'll be alright."

The tone of his voice didn't match the confidence of his words.

"But what if it attacks her?" she asked.

"She's a mile away by..."

He paused peering at a spot in the darkness and suddenly the desert night exploded with a snarl. Quicker than the eye can follow, the beast sprang out of the darkness, Avery's rifle rang out but the wolf knocked Avery to the ground and leaped towards Andrew.

Andrew tried to bring his rifle around but the wolf was on him before he could fire. He fell back to the ground, with the creature bearing down on him. Its long yellow teeth snapping at his throat.

The length of the rifle pushing against the wolf's neck was the only thing keeping those teeth from sinking into Andrew's jugular. Its paws and their long claws raked at Andrew's arms and chest trying to reach him, slicing his skin to ribbons. Andrew tried to lock his elbows but the weight of the carnivore bore down on him.

"He's too heavy! I can't hold him!"

Avery scrambled to his feet, bringing up his rifle, but he didn't fire for fear of hitting Andrew. He moved quickly to the side but still couldn't get a clear shot. Kaya stood frozen watching in horror as the animal continued to slice at Andrew, snarling, drool spilling down over the neck it yearned to sink its teeth into.

"Somebody shoot the damn thing!" screamed Andrew through clenched teeth.

"I can't hold him... much... longer."

Andrew's arms were on fire and the pain magnified with each swipe of the vicious claws. He ached to move his arms away from those claws but he knew if he did so, he'd be dead. Kaya frozen by the scene before her looked down at the revolver in her hands, the one Avery had handed her, and then back to Andrew, covered in blood. She pulled the hammer back with her thumb and raised the pistol with both hands, aiming at the face of the demon from her dream. As she did so, the wolf raised its head to her. As her finger tightened on the trigger, the wolf gave a low growl and was in the air, leaping towards her. Time froze as her finger squeezed, the trigger moved, and the hammer came down.

The bullet exited the barrel of the pistol silently. It floated, spiraling through the air, and met fur, pushing its way through, searing past skin, fat, and a thin muscle. It met a bone and pushed on it until it splintered. The bullet changed direction then, angling to the right, skimming along the edge of a lung, slicing through more tissue. It traveled through different organs, the stomach, and lower intestines, floating like a hot knife through butter. Then it met a dark mass, the liver, and easily glided through it, hot blood filling the void behind it. It came to another bone, this one harder and thicker, much stronger. It pushed and cracked the bone once again, but it had slowed and a large chunk of the bullet was left there embedded. The rest of the bullet continued through another bit of muscle and then fat to find itself pushing against skin once again. The skin stretched outward until it could stretch no more and the bullet tore through, taking with it a spray of blood droplets and fur. It soared through the air out into the darkness, followed by the echoing boom of its sound finally catching up with it. Gliding through the air, dropping lower and lower, catching the top of a sagebrush, then the trunk of another, eventually skidding to a stop, the bullet buried itself into the dirt, to wait, unmoving, for years, until the flows of the earth reclaimed it, but then bullets aren't bothered by such things.

The wolf landed on Kaya, pinning her to the ground. Her heart stopped and her breath caught in her throat. Andrew rolled over scrambling to his feet, kicking at the ground, willing himself to get to Kaya. Avery reached her first and stopped. Neither the wolf nor she was moving. Everything was eerily still. Andrew dropped his gun and pulled at the tuft of the wolf's neck, Avery quickly grabbed a leg and helped drag the mass of stinking fur off of her. Kaya lay unmoving, eyes wide open, her skin pale in the firelight. She looked very much dead to Avery and Andrew's eyes. Andrew dropped to his knees and cupped her face in his hands.

"Kaya!"

For a split second nothing happened, and then with a great force, Kaya sucked in a breath of air and looked around in bewilderment, pushing with her feet she struggled to get up. Her heart raced and her lungs sucked for air they didn't think was there.

"Kaya! It's okay. I've got you. Sit back and just breathe."

Andrew gripped her arms, as she hyperventilated, trying to keep her from sprinting off into the darkness.

"Kaya, breath. You're okay.

Andrew squeezed her arms harder to get her to focus on him. Her eyes darted and finally met his and she held them there. She nodded and after a few moments, her breathing began to slow.

Andrew sat down and held her, rubbing her back in long smooth strokes. Avery brought his canteen, but Andrew held up his hand.

"Wait on that for a bit. Let her catch her breath."

On a camping trip, Andrew remembered his dad telling him that shock can kill a person and that the best thing to do is lay them down, get their breathing under control, and keep them warm. Never give them food or water, he was clear about that. His dad always wanted him to know how to handle things if anything ever happened while the two of them were in the wilderness. The only other thing he recalled him telling him to do for shock was to get help and call for an ambulance.

I don't see many of those around.

The main thing was to keep them warm and breathing, Andrew remembered. He moved around and let Kaya lay down next to the fire, her head resting in his lap. He looked her up and down for any wounds, but he saw none. The only blood on her was what had smeared off of his lacerated arms and chest. He felt her skin, it was cool and clammy.

Shit.

"Avery hand me that coat over there and then throw a few more chunks on the fire if you wouldn't mind."

Andrew tried to keep his voice calm, he thought it might make it worse if Kaya knew he was worried. Avery handed him the coat and built the fire back up to a steady roar, without a word. He could tell something was wrong.

"Kaya... how do you feel?"

Andrew did his best to keep his voice calm.

"Col... cold," she whispered.

Andrew began rubbing his hands up and down over her arms, trying to warm her.

"Kaya, tell Avery how to start a fire with a bow and drill. He doesn't know how."

"In the morning."

"No, he wants to know now, so that he can restart the fire in the morning if it goes out."

"Tell him not to let the bottom slip."

Her voice was barely audible, but Andrew saw a hint of a smile.

"Very funny little lady. Come on now tell him, he needs to know, otherwise, we won't have a warm fire in the morning and you'll have to light it."

When she didn't reply, fear iced over his heart. He gently slapped the side of her face with his fingers.

"Kaya!"

Her eyes fluttered open and she stared up at him, a distant glassy look in her eyes.

"First take off your boots for the laces to make your bow..."

Her voice trailed off and her eyes drifted shut.

"Kaya? Kaya!"

Tears brimmed in Andrew's eyes as he held Kaya's face in his hands. Avery came over and picked up her hand, softly pinching her wrist between his thumb and forefinger.

"Her pulse is weak but it's steady. She may just need some sleep. We can take turns watching her breathing, make sure it doesn't..."

Avery trailed off.

"It's alright, I'll watch her. I'm not going to sleep while she's like this," said Andrew without taking his eyes off her face.

Andrew bent over and kissed her forehead. He sniffed and wiped his nose with the back of his hand. Avery nodded, knowing there was no use in arguing. He looked over at the still body of the wolf lying only a single stride from Andrew and Kaya. Grabbing it by the legs, he dragged the large furry mass out into the darkness away from their camp. When he returned, Andrew looked up and smiled halfheartedly.

"Thanks."

"Sure. I... I'm sorry I froze back there. If I would have just shot this never would have happened."

"No, it's alright. I wouldn't have taken the shot either, would have been too risky."

"Yeah, but still, I thought I would've... I dunno... reacted better in a situation like that."

"It's okay. It's not easy to know what to do, most of the time I don't. Maybe sometimes I've been right or maybe sometimes I have just been lucky... I don't know. But I do know... I'm tired of watching people die."

Avery nodded.

"We should get you patched up. You're still bleeding."

Andrew said nothing and just stared ahead, out into the black night, but Avery imagined what Andrew was seeing was a different kind of darkness.

CHAPTER 17
THE OASIS

THE SMOKE *of the sagebrush gives off a scent much different than that of woodsmoke. It's an exotic spice, something foreign you wouldn't expect in the deserts of the West. It's an allure, a beckoning of wild spirits and ancient ghosts to join your camp once the sun has fallen and gone. Spirits seeking out lost souls, the ones that the West has drawn to her bosom for the last few centuries. The souls that hear her call, her promise of the wild, the danger, the opportunity; those that abandon civilization for the wild woman that is the West. She whispers in their ear at the rising of the sun, she taunts, teases--come find me. Ever do they search, but the woman can't be found, they give up their souls to find her, for that is the price she demands. She takes but she does not give, like a widow in its web.*

These soulless hearts spend their nights beside the fire of the burning sage and welcome the ghosts, for they are good company, they are the only company. The soulless heart shares his stories of the West, and how she has taken all that he was and is. The ghosts listen in sorrow. They know the story, for it is theirs. They beckon the heart with no soul to join them, because they are the same and their soulless journey is the same. So the heart goes, because he has nothing left, and in the rising dawn, the spice of the smoke from the fire is all that remains.

The fire spit sparks at Andrew as he added another dry branch. He sat in front of the blaze, glancing upward at the night sky. He could just make out the horizon of the mountains in the distance. The sun would be up soon. Already he could see the gray outlines of the sagebrush beyond the light of the fire. He was still shaken from his dream. A woman smelling of spice had stolen everything he had and ghosts had come to take him away, but the details faded away like a candle flickering on its last bit of wick.

He was angry; he had fallen asleep sometime in the night. He had checked on Kaya as soon as he woke, and her breathing had been steady and normal, but he was still upset with himself. Kaya could have needed him. He picked up a pebble and threw it hard, venting his frustration. He heard it land in the water with a small plop, as the current swept it away. He needed to walk, to relax. Chewing his fingers off wasn't doing Kaya any good. He stood up, flexing his tingling legs. He walked out following the river to the south. He watched the water rush over the rocks and slow to a crawl at the deep wide sections, where the current was weakest, and the edges formed spinning eddies. He stumbled twice over the large round river rocks and angled over into the sagebrush and the soft-packed rabbit trails.

A light breeze pushed through his coat and he shivered, wishing he had brought his hat. He wondered to himself why it was always coldest before the dawn. Why is it that in the minutes before the warmth of the sun bathes the landscape the temperature drops to its coldest? He saw a glowing line at the top of the mountains to the west, making them look like they were on fire. The fire slowly spread down to the bottom of the mountain, illuminating it in gold. Then it crawled across the valley floor, like a slow tidal wave coming for him. He turned to the dark horizon of mountains to the east and watched as a bright diamond formed where the sky met the peaks. The diamond grew in size and intensity, and then with an explosion of blinding light, the tidal wave washed over him. He felt the warmth on his face as he stood there with his eyes closed tight against the white light of the sun.

He took a couple of deep breaths. The cold morning air bit at his nostrils as it rushed down into his lungs.

This is good.

He could feel the stress leaving his body as the sun continued to rise, warming his spirit. He let out a long slow breath and opened his eyes. He was ready for whatever this day was going to bring down on him. He turned back to camp and made his way following the zigzag of rabbit trails. A shrill cry rang out in the still morning air. He froze, listening.

"No! Get off! Ahhh! Get away!"

Kaya.

Andrew ran, dodging the sagebrush, sprinting when he could. He leaped through a large clump of brush and caught his foot, nearly falling into camp. Andrew's eyes raced back and forth looking for the threat.

In the middle of the camp, standing over Kaya was Avery's horse, doing her absolute best to cover Kaya's face in horse slobber. She licked and nibbled with her lips while Kaya desperately tried pushing her away. She was spitting, obviously Bonnie had gotten her mouth.

Andrew couldn't help it, he burst out in laughter, relief washing over him. Avery was up, moving to take hold of Bonnie, but he was having trouble controlling his amusement as well. He grabbed her by the halter and pulled her away from Kaya.

"Glad you two are enjoying yourselves!" said Kaya with a glare as she sat up, wiping her face with her arm.

"I'm sorry, I heard your screams and I thought... but when I got here and saw..."

Kaya grinned and nodded. Andrew came over and sat beside her, wrapping her in his arms.

"I'm just glad you're alright. I was really worried about you," he said squeezing her tight.

She smiled and turned to meet his lips with hers when Avery interrupted.

"It's true, he was up all night watching over you."

Avery had his back to them, rubbing down Bonnie with her blanket and checking her for injuries. Kaya turned back to Andrew and gave him a look of pure adoration. She leaned in and kissed him, her hand coming up to the back of his neck and her fingers pushing up through his hair. She stopped abruptly.

"Oh, sorry. I really gotta pee."

She scrambled up and disappeared into the sagebrush before Andrew could utter a word.

"Uh... fine. It was kind of like kissing a girl covered in horse slobber anyway!"

Avery chuckled. Andrew stood and walked over to him and Bonnie. He scratched her head and straightened the bit of mane that spilled out between her ears.

"Is she alright?" asked Andrew.

"Yeah, I think so. A few scratches, but nothing bad."

They were both silent for a moment, each lost in their thoughts, while Bonnie enjoyed the scratching of the two men. Avery picked up the saddle and swung it over her back.

"Well, shall we hit the trail? We should be able to make it to the ranch in an hour, maybe two. I'll cook us up a hot meal and you two can shower and relax for a bit."

"Avery, you have no idea how good that sounds. We can't thank you enough."

"Don't mention it, besides like I said, I've been stuck out here alone for damn near a year. I could use the company."

Kaya returned, wrapping her arm around Andrew's waist, and smiled at them.

"Well, boys what are we talking about?"

Andrew just stared down at her smiling face and realized just how worried he had been that he might lose her.

"Breakfast back at the ranch. As long as you feel fit to travel," said Avery.

"Awe, I can't wait. I'd walk a thousand miles for a real meal."

"Well that's good, but you don't have to walk. Bonnie here would be glad to give you a ride. The least she can do after waking you up with wet horse kisses."

"Really? I've never ridden a horse before. This is great. Okay, how do I get on?"

Avery guided her to the side and helped her get her foot into the stirrup, then once on showed her how to sit and how to control Bonnie using the reins.

"You shouldn't have to do much, she's like a big puppy and will just follow me along, but if something happens to spook her I want you to be able to stop her. You ready?"

Kaya nodded excitedly. Andrew walked back to the smoldering fire to collect their things. Avery had already collected his pot and the tin cans. Andrew picked up his rifle and pistol, securing it back in its charred holster. Donning his fur hat he motioned to Avery that he was all set. He glanced through the brush at the body of the massive gray wolf and hoped that would be the last of the creatures he'd ever see.

"Alright, cowgirl, let's head out!"

Kaya was nearly hopping with excitement as Avery walked ahead leading Bonnie. Andrew followed behind laughing, the stiffness in his strained muscles working out with each step. His heart was high, knowing that soon they'd be safe at Avery's ranch, with the comforts and amenities of a home, a real home. It had been so long that Andrew had nearly forgotten what a home meant. It was safety, it was comfort. It was something to keep the wolves at bay.

———

A chill of sheer ecstasy enveloped her body as the hot water cascaded down her back. Kaya had never seen such dirty water rush down a drain. She scrubbed at her skin relentlessly with the bar of soap, feeling that she would never be completely clean again. She stayed under the near-scalding water until the solar bag shriveled into a flat piece of plastic.

Kaya pushed her hair back out of her face and ran her hands over the back of her head, squeezing the water from it. Stepping from the tub, she retrieved the crisp, folded towel. She relished in the scent and the feel of the cotton as it brushed the dampness from her body.

There was a comb in the cabinet behind the mirror and she began the assault on the knots that had started to form a nest in her hair. She tugged and pulled for nearly twenty minutes and finally decided it would have to do. Any more and she'd be pulling all her hair out. She looked in the mirror. She hardly recognized the person staring back at her. She was older looking, leaner than she remembered, and there were lines at her eyes and her mouth where there hadn't been before. She turned and began to dress. Avery had been kind enough to let her pick out clothes from his sister's closet. She had picked out something with Andrew in mind and her hands shook in excitement and fear to see the look on his face when he saw her.

After having fed and watered Bonnie, Avery started working on something to feed them. He built a fire in a large cast-iron stove that looked like it was at least a century old. Andrew watched as he pulled a white package out of a large chest freezer, set it aside, and then disappeared out the back door. He returned a moment later holding up the bottom of his shirt and packing something. He strode to the counter where he deposited an enormous amount of eggs.

"You've got chickens?"

"Yup! A mess of 'em. They think they're pretty smart with their hiding spots but I am always one step ahead of them. Oh shit, I'm getting ahead of myself. We're missing the most important part of the meal!"

He whipped open a cabinet door and pulled out a tall tin pot and a lid.

"Coffee?" asked Avery with a grin.

"Absolutely!"

Avery was about to say something else but when Andrew turned suddenly, he stopped. Standing in the doorway was Kaya, dressed in a yellow sun dress that fit surprisingly well. She smiled but cast her eyes down, somewhat embarrassed by the attention.

Andrew sat with his mouth agape, speechless. Avery looked from one to the other and felt if nobody was going to say anything he was going to have to.

"Looking good, Kaya. Clothes fit okay?"

"Thank you very much, and yes they fit perfectly. Glad somebody notices."

This snapped Andrew's jaw shut and knocked him out of his stupor. He stood quickly to defend himself.

"It's not that, I was speechless. I can't believe how pretty you look."

"Gee, thanks."

"No, you know what I mean. I've never seen you in a dress. You look... beautiful."

Kaya walked up to him, her bare feet creaking the old wood floor.

"Why, thank you," she said as she wrapped her arms around his neck and embraced him in a passionate kiss.

After a moment Andrew pulled back, looking at her and then down at himself.

"And I am filthy, stinky, and probably getting your dress dirty."

Avery had busied himself with their meal with his back to them but turned pointing to the front door.

"If you're ready for a shower, grab one of the bags off the front porch and help yourself. There should be another towel in there. Breakfast...er lunch should be ready when you get out."

"I think I'll do that," said Andrew pulling away.

He started to go but took her face in his hands and kissed her again.

"You are so beautiful," he whispered on her lips.

Kaya blushed, but smiled, biting her lip and holding his gaze. Andrew kissed her once more and disappeared out the front door only to reappear seconds later hefting a large sloshing black bag with a hose coming out the bottom.

"You're going to love it!" called out Kaya as he made his way to the bathroom.

Kaya went outside to explore and to enjoy the autumn sun. It was warm, not exactly sundress warm, but she didn't care. The look in Andrew's eyes had made it worth it.

She ventured out to the corrals where there were six horses standing side by side, nose to tail, each one looked so close to sleeping that they'd topple over, causing a domino effect. The only thing that gave any indication of their alertness was their swishing tails. Each tail swung side to side brushing the face of the horse next to it. With each swing of the wiry tails, a mass of flies would lift off the horse's necks only to land again when the coast was clear. It was an odd symphony, a perfectly coordinated ballet of aggravation and reprisal.

One of the horse's ears perked when Kaya leaned on the weathered wood of the fence rail. It quickly turned, leaving the line-up, and walked up to Kaya. It was Bonnie. She stopped with her head near Kaya so that she could get scratched and was close enough to receive a treat without the others knowing if that's what this nice human was here for.

Kaya scratched her head and petted the soft skin of her nose. Bonnie closed her eyes. Soon the other horses grew curious or jealous and approached the fence and each received their fair share of attention. After a while, Kaya turned to leave, having given Bonnie one extra scratch. The horses watched her go, having now formed a new fly removal line next to the fence.

Kaya worked her way through the backyard shaded by massive trees, a sight she didn't expect to see in the desert. There was even a small stream flowing through the yard, coming off of the hillside to the back of the house.

"This is like an oasis. No wonder Avery has managed so well out here alone," she said to herself.

The thought of being alone for such a long time, even in this place, made her shiver. Her nose caught a familiar, devilish smell. One that was a bane to many who struggled to give up meat and live the life of a vegetarian. It was the smell of bacon. Her stomach growled so loud a chicken sprang from the bush next to her, running for its life. Kaya snorted as she laughed at the puffed-up chicken, wings out, skittering away to the next bush.

Again her belly growled and her stomach felt like an empty pit. So, she let her nose lead her back to the quaint old farmhouse. Inside it was a sizzling steam house of pans clanging and dishes rattling. Avery was moving quickly from pan to pan, stirring this and flipping that.

"Avery? Is there anything I can do?"

"Save your breath. I already asked. He's determined to play host."

Andrew was leaning in the doorway to the kitchen and Kaya hardly recognized him. Avery had given him some of his clothes to wear, a pair of jeans and a button-up western-style shirt. The shirt was un-tucked and he had his thumb stuck into the pocket of his jeans. Kaya couldn't take her eyes off him. She walked up to him, sliding her arms past his waist and wrapping him in a hug.

"My, don't you clean up good? I'm not sure what to think of it, I assumed I was living with a mountain man all this time."

"And I thought I was living with a wild druid girl. I guess we are both disappointed."

Andrew laughed but Kaya pulled back and slapped his chest, pretending to be hurt. She sat down at the kitchen table with glaring eyes but her wide smile gave her away.

"Whoops! I'm sorry. I totally forgot."

Avery pulled two heavy white mugs from a cabinet and filled them with a dark liquid from the pot on the stove. He brought them over to the table as Andrew sat down next to Kaya. The tantalizing scent of freshly brewed coffee nearly made Andrew's head spin.

"Thank you so much, Avery, this is… this is awesome."

"You're welcome, I hope you like it black. I just used up the last of the sugar in the gravy, and I haven't gotten around to milking Jezebel yet."

"You have your own milk cow?" squealed Kaya.

"Of course. I couldn't live without my butter and my cheese!"

He smiled but quickly turned back to his un-chaperoned kitchen.

"This place is so cool," Kaya said to Andrew.

But she didn't get a reply. Andrew was lost in a euphoria, savoring the scent of the fresh ground slow-roasted beans.

"Should I leave you alone with your cup for a while?" She snickered.

Andrew came to, but before he could reply Avery laid down a pan of plump golden biscuits and a pot of what looked like chocolate pudding. Andrew and Kaya's mouths watered at the sight.

"I don't know if you guys have ever had biscuits and

chocolate gravy before but I think you'll like it. Like I said it used the last of the sugar, and I have been saving the last of the cocoa for a special occasion, but I think this qualifies!"

He quickly returned with a massive cast iron pan, carried by two mitten-covered hands, full of dark orange lumps.

"Are those scrambled eggs?" asked Kaya.

"Yup!" said Avery beaming.

"Are they always that color?" asked Kaya.

Avery laughed.

"Yes, as long as they are loose and free to eat what they'd naturally eat. The yellow eggs you might be used to were from caged, corn-fed, sick chickens. Yolks are naturally orange; they are yellow when the chicken lacks nutrition."

"Wow! I had no idea," exclaimed Kaya.

Avery chuckled again.

"That's why all those chickens got wiped out so easily, lack of nutrition, kept in dark warehouses, pumped full of antibiotics and hormones to make them grow more meat."

"Oh, that's horrible!"

"It's the same with the dairies and feed lots. The cows standing in two feet of their own shit, pumped full of drugs to keep them from getting sick, having corn stuffed down their throats to make them fatter, and... and this isn't a very good conversation to have before we eat. Sorry about that. I tend to fly off the handle. But don't worry; this is all home-grown, natural, healthy, drug-free food."

Avery seemed to think for a moment.

"Now no that's not exactly true. The chickens did get into my grow house, so I can't exactly say drug-free," he said.

Kaya and Andrew looked at each other.

"Pot? You mean you grow pot?"

Andrew was a little bewildered.

"Sure do. No reason not to, nowadays. It's medicinal," he said with a wink.

With a yelp, Avery jumped up and retrieved a plate full of glistening bacon.

"Almost forgot the second best part," he said stuffing a strip into his mouth.

He passed the plate to Andrew, whose eyes opened wide at the sight.

"Kaya, no bacon for you, I'm assuming?" Said Avery.

"No thank you! Besides, there's enough food here to eat for a week."

Kaya and Andrew couldn't remember the last time they had had such a divine meal. However, well before they had managed to put a dent in it, they were both stretched back in their chairs doing their best not to pass out.

"It's so good and I don't want to leave any, but I... just can't," whimpered Kaya.

"I guess we have gotten used to eating a lot less. I can't hold another scrap," said Andrew.

"Not to worry, I'll put it up and we will have the rest for supper. I'll bet you two could use some rest. I can show you to your room, it's not always a good idea to sleep right after a big meal, but it's up to you. You both look dead tired."

He didn't get a response as both their eyelids seemed to droop lower.

"Come on. I'll show you to your suite. When you two are fresh, then we can talk business."

Neither knew what that meant, but they were too tired to ask. They followed him like drones to their room. It was simple but cozy. A bed covered in a colorful quilt with a wooden headboard, a small dresser, and a chair in the corner.

"Sweet dreams! Let me know if you need anything," hollered Avery as he closed the door.

Andrew and Kaya smiled at each other and slid into the bed, sinking into the comfort of the mattress, wrapping their arms around one another, not even bothering to pull the covers back. In moments they were both sound asleep.

———

Avery sat on the porch, rocking back and forth in an old creaking chair, watching as the light on the mountains changed from gold to purple as the sun got nearer to setting.

Andrew stepped out onto the porch yawning and stretching. His overgrown hair matted in some spots and shooting out in others.

"Well, good morning sleepy head. Or should I say good evening? How did you sleep?"

"Like a ton of bricks, I suppose. It was fantastic," said Andrew yawning again.

"Well here, pull up a seat."

Avery motioned to the rocker next to him.

Andrew sat down running his hands over the time-worn wood, faded and smooth. He leaned back in it, lifting his bare heels, rocking back and forth. He followed Avery's gaze to the mountains.

"This is a beautiful spot."

"Sure is. Shame..."

"Huh?"

"Shame that I'm not gonna be able to enjoy it for much longer. That's what I wanted to talk about, but it would be better if Kaya were here, too. This concerns both of you."

"I'm here," said Kaya softly, who had suddenly appeared at the doorway.

"Did I wake you when I got up?" Asked Andrew.

"Yeah, but I am glad I got up before the sunset. Always weird to fall asleep during the day and wake up in the middle of the night."

Kaya shuffled to the edge of the porch and sat at the edge in front of Andrew wrapping her arm around the post, gazing at the mountains.

"Well good. Since you're both up, now seems like the right time."

Avery stopped for a moment and reached over to the table next to him. He picked up something small and a box of matches. It looked like a cigarette but Andrew quickly realized it was a joint.

With the joint between his lips, Avery struck a match. The match illuminated the lines of his face as he held the flame to the tip until it was glowing red. He took a heavy drag and held the smoke and vapor in his lungs for a moment. As he exhaled, he tilted his back against the chair and rocked easily.

"I'm leaving, headed for South America. This is my home and I love it here, but we can't stay. You see when the power went out every nuclear power plant in the world went on backup generators, to keep the plutonium and what-not cool. If the rods are not kept cool, they superheat and essentially melt through everything."

He paused for effect.

"Everything," he repeated.

"Radiation will pollute the ground and burn up into the atmosphere. North America will be dead. No trees, no plants, no birds, no nothing. There are over fifty nuclear power plants in the US. Most of them are east of the Rockies, but there's enough scattered around here on the west coast to kill everything within the next few years, once those generators start running out of fuel. There are three nuclear plants in South America as far as I know and all three are located in the central part of the continent. So there are two safe zones, to the north in the Amazon and way, way south to the peninsula. Tierra del Fuego, that's where I'm heading. It's not going to be an easy trip, but that's where you two come in. You seem like good enough people, strong, smart. I don't think I can make this trip alone. I want you to come with me. We can watch each other's backs; keep each other going, when the going gets tough. Fight off thieves and such. Power in numbers you know?"

Andrew's heart was pounding. If what he was saying was

true, life as he now knew it was about to dramatically change, again. No life north of the equator. Maybe the world really was coming to an end.

"I know it's a lot to take in, but I don't see that you have got much of a choice. The only other option you have is to head north, way north. Arctic Circle territory and I don't know about you but I'm not too crazy about meeting a polar bear. I know you're headed to your uncle's, I understand. Family is important, whatever is left of it. If you can convince them to come, that's fine. But, I've only got so many horses and so much food. They'd have to contribute."

Andrew's mind reeled with a flood of emotions and worry. He knew Avery was right. There wasn't a choice, they had to go. But, still, he couldn't wrap his mind around leaving his country, his home, and his parents. The memory stabbed at him suddenly and he felt sick, thinking of the bodies of his parents, probably still lying there on the patio, hands clutching. He wished badly that he could give them a proper burial. His eyes watered and he did his best to push the memories down and blink away the tears.

"I'll need some time..."

Andrew's voice cracked, betraying his attempt at stifling his feelings. He cleared his throat.

"I need to find my family first and if I can convince them, we'll come with you," said Andrew, his voice steadier.

"Good, you've got time. I'm not leaving 'til the spring. I've still got lots of prepping to do."

Avery lit the joint again and took another hit. He coughed this time as he blew out the gray smoke.

"I'm sorry. How rude of me," he croaked.

He leaned over handing the joint to Andrew, along with the box of matches. Andrew started to refuse but took it, looking down at the fragile joint. Andrew had never smoked and he was a little nervous, but for the life of him, he couldn't come up with a good reason not to. He stuck the tip to his lips and struck a match, his fumbling fingers breaking the match. The lit end fell into his lap, and he jumped up swatting at the flame. Avery belted out a laugh slapping his knee and nearly coming out of his chair. Kaya even exploded in a fit of laughter.

Andrew scowled but couldn't keep the sides of his mouth from curling. It was funny he had to admit. He sat back down and struck another match, more carefully this time. He held the round flame to the tip of the cigarette and inhaled deeply. He didn't feel anything at first, and then all at once his lungs were on fire. He jerked the joint out of his mouth and began coughing harshly as he felt the heat of the smoke rush back out of his lungs. Avery began howling once again. Andrew handed the joint and matches to Kaya, struggling to stifle his coughs, which only seemed to make it worse.

Kaya took the small cigarette from him and examined it. She put it between her lips and took a hit, holding it for a moment and then blowing out the smoke with barely a cough.

With a bit of surprise, Andrew realized that she had probably done this before, but he was still too busy trying to stifle his coughs to worry about it. Finally, the burning in his lungs and throat seemed to calm him. He sat back in his chair, closing his eyes. Despite the coughing fit, he felt lighter and more relaxed than he'd been in years. He felt the earth giving way beneath him and he snapped open his eyes, certain he was falling. But everything was still. The sun had finally gone down and darkness was settling in.

Andrew lifted his hand to his face, moving it back and forth. In the fading light, his hand was a blur of movement even though he was moving it rather slowly.

Funny, must be a trick of the light.

He leaned his head back once again, thoroughly enjoying the rhythmic rocking of the chair.

"Well, I think this calls for a celebration. I don't get to have guests very often."

Avery pulled another drag from the joint and then disappeared into the house. When he returned he was burdened with an arm full of items, none of which Andrew could identify in the dark. Avery made his way back to his chair, depositing his load into it, and then began fiddling with something on the far porch post. He struck a match and the porch illuminated in golden light as he lit a hanging lantern. He turned and removed, what Andrew could now see was a guitar and a glass mason jar from his chair and sat down. Spinning the ring off the jar and prying up the lid with his fingernails, he took a large gulp and passed it to Andrew. Andrew took it hesitantly; already feeling rather intoxicated from the marijuana. He stared at the dark contents suspiciously.

"Is it... moonshine?"

"God, no. That shit's nasty. Nope, that there is homemade apple brandy. About two years old. Sure to please even the most particular of palettes."

Avery smiled to himself proudly.

Andrew took a cautious sip, the sweet liquor gliding past his tongue and down the back of his throat. It warmed his chest and belly.

"This is delicious. You made this?"

"Why thank you. It was my grandpa's recipe."

Avery picked up his guitar and plucked at the strings, listening and then adjusting the knobs until it was tuned to his liking. Andrew took another drink and passed the jar to Kaya. Kaya tilted the jar back and spilled a little down her chin. She swallowed trying hard not to laugh as she wiped her face with the back of her hand. She set the jar down and laughed, also feeling the weed. She looked up at Andrew. He beamed down at her, and they stared into each other's eyes.

"Well now, let's see, how about Wagon Wheel? A little Old Crow Medicine Show?"

Avery started strumming a tune and Andrew and Kaya slowly moved with the rhythm, Andrew tapping his foot and Kaya swaying back and forth.

Andrew jumped to his feet and leaped from the porch. The effects of the marijuana and brandy made him a little unsteady but he held his ground. He reached out for Kaya's hand, grinning from ear to ear.

"What? Dance? You want me to dance?!"

"Oh go on Kaya. This is what we're here for ain't it? Tonight might be our last night on earth," said Avery, picking up the next verse.

Kaya dropped her head in defeat and allowed herself to be led out onto the gravel. Long shadows stretched from the porch posts across the yard as Andrew took her by the waist with his right hand and held her hand up with his left. They danced around laughing and spinning as the weight of the world fell away.

CHAPTER 18
LEFT ALONE

KAYA BOUNCED up and down as Bonnie trotted up the small hill. Andrew followed slowly behind on his horse, Duke, a stocky buckskin whose sole purpose in life was to nibble at grass along the trail.

They had stayed with Avery on his ranch for nearly a week and had spent the days helping him with the various chores and enjoying the comforts of a real home.

Yesterday, Andrew had decided it was time to get moving. When he told Avery where his uncle's ranch was, Avery had turned very somber and seemed as though he wanted to say something, but he didn't. He just pulled out a map and showed Andrew the route to get there. It happened to be the next valley to the east, a distance of twenty or thirty miles, with a small range of hills to cross.

So Avery loaded them up with supplies, enough for a few days, and gave them the horses. Andrew was hesitant about taking the horses, he knew they could travel faster with them, but he, like Kaya, had never ridden before. He voiced his concerns but Avery was confident in the two horses he had picked out for them.

"They're bulletproof, just point 'em in the right direction

and set the autopilot. You'll be fine. I've showed you guys enough on how to rein, and how to get 'em stopped if they run away with ya. But the secret to riding is getting a rhythm with the animal, your rear will thank you."

Nudging Andrew in the ribs, he continued in a hushed tone.

"So here's the thing, when you're riding, especially in a trot or a gallop, you move your hips to the rhythm of the horse like you're making love to a beautiful woman. Trust me."

Avery's grin was wider than his hat brim.

Avery's advice was good, and it helped a lot but after riding all morning Andrew was beginning to get sore none-theless. Kaya, however, seemed at home on a horse. She and Bonnie were making zigzags around him; exploring this and that, while he and his mini Clydesdale of a buckskin plodded slowly along.

About an hour from Avery's ranch, they came to the high-way. It was eerily placid. The asphalt was gray from layers of dust. Weeds had grown up through the cracks of the neglected road. They turned and followed the highway north. They counted the mile markers and took the dirt road to the right after the fifth one. Avery said that road would take them through the hills and into the next valley.

A few hours later, they stopped in a pass protected from the frigid wind by short shrubby trees growing next to a small creek. The banks of the creek, where the current was the slowest had ice along its edges. They were both thankful for the new coats Avery had supplied them with.

After loosening the strap on his saddle, Andrew removed a jar of bright orange peaches and a fork from his saddle bags. Kaya was still brushing down Bonnie and scratching her neck. Andrew sat on a rock, warm from the sun, and popped open the jar. He stabbed one of the slices and stuffed it into his mouth, the sweet juice dripping down his chin.

"Wamm sum peeshes?" He managed, as he scarfed down another piece of the decadent fruit.

"Yes please."

Kaya skipped playfully over to him, grinning like a schoolgirl.

She plopped down next to him. He handed her the jar and smiled, having gulped down the last of his slice. She took the jar but then she hesitated. She stared into his brown eyes with a crooked smile. He was about to say something when she leaned in and licked the juice from his chin. The look on Andrew's dumbfounded face was too much to take and she burst out laughing. But she stopped when the look went from shock to embarrassment. She grasped the back of his head and pulled him to her, attacking his lips with hers. When they separated, they were both breathing deeply and a wicked smile crossed her lips.

"Not that I'm complaining, but what has gotten into you?"

"I'm happy. I am happy to be here. I'm happy to be alive and I am happy to be with you!"

She smiled and kissed his cheek and then stabbed a peach slice with the fork and stuffed it in her mouth. Andrew just smiled and shook his head. The wind picked up through the little pass, shaking the brown leaves off the branches of the little trees.

"Here--"

Kaya was holding a slice out to him. He opened and she pushed it into his mouth.

"Tanks," he murmured, chewing.

The cold wind bit at his exposed ears. He pulled a sock cap Avery had given him from his pocket and pulled it down over his head since Kaya had taken to wearing his fur hat. She had tried to give it back several times, but Andrew could tell she liked it, and he had to admit she looked pretty darn cute in it.

They finished up the jar of peaches, drinking down the

sweet juice, then Andrew rinsed the jar at the stream and stowed it back in his saddle bags. Then they tightened their saddles once again and continued on.

They followed the dirt road most of the time but in places it had been washed out so bad that it was impassable and they had to go around. Deep flood-formed gorges ran down the center of the road in most places.

They crested a small hill and the scene before them stopped them in their tracks. Black rolling hills stretched out in front of them. The sage was burned nearly down to the ground like frayed ends of cable writhing up through the ash-covered soil. The blackened landscape stretched for miles in all directions.

"What caused it do you think?" asked Kaya pulling the flaps of the hat down over her ears.

"I don't know. Lightning maybe."

The wind howled across their path, taking every bit of the black dust that the hooves of the horses kicked up. They rode with their heads tilted to the side trying to keep the icy daggers of the wind off their necks.

It seemed as though they rode for days, weeks even, the unchanging desolation of the landscape and the deafening wind lulled them both into a somber trance as they plodded along, Kaya and Bonnie having lost their usual spring.

It was late afternoon when the horses slowed to a stop. Both Andrew and Kaya had been lost in a melancholy of memories, distant memories that no longer carried the painful stab of emotion, just a numb tingling of regrets and words never said. They both lifted their heads against the wind, seeing what had caused the horses to stop. They were at the edge of a steep bluff. But what stopped Andrew's heart, was the valley that lay beyond. Once lush green fields that had carpeted the small valley now were stained black with ash.

With a heavy sinking feeling, the realization struck that

the last of Andrew's family was gone. There was no way someone could be living down there, if by chance they escaped the fire, they were long gone. Still, he had to see it with his eyes. They made their way down the hill following the winding road, past shells and foundations that were once homes, and twisted masses of metal shops and barns. Trucks and tractors, blackened with soot, stood silent like ancient grave markers.

Andrew reined up his horse when they came to a mailbox on a metal wagon wheel, still standing waiting for its post. He looked beyond it. Where once his uncle's house had stood was nothing, except for the spindly skeletons of two tall trees. Trees he and his cousins had climbed in; where his uncle had tied a rope to one of the branches to make a tire swing for them.

When they reached the debris of the home, Andrew slid from his horse and slowly walked up to the remnants of a charred and melted tire lying beneath the tree.

He sank to his knees and broke down. He cried. He cried for his aunt and uncle, he cried for Jupiter, he cried for Lee, he cried for Mrs. Owens, and he cried for his parents. He had lost everyone, except one, and she was there, kneeling in front of him, wrapping her arms around him. Shedding her own tears; for the pain of the world had been left to them, to bear alone.

EPILOGUE

THE DAY HAD COME. Spring was beginning to show signs of its arrival. The birds were returning, and the geese flew high overhead, loudly announcing their approach long before their majestic pattern could be spotted against the pale blue sky. The snow and the icy streams had thawed, and the trees in the yard of the small ranch house were beginning to bud.

Andrew, Kaya, and Avery had spent the last four months gathering all the food and supplies they would need to start the journey. Now it was all packed on the horses, six in all: three to ride; three with pack saddles.

Avery did one final walk through his home, taking in every memory he could. He started to lock the door behind him, but he stopped himself. Maybe a cold traveler would find it, or his parents by some miracle could still be alive and make it back to read the note he had left for them on the table.

He pulled the door closed softly until it latched and then picked up the soft nylon guitar case off the porch and pulled the straps over his shoulders. Andrew and Kaya were sitting on their horses, waiting. Kaya's belly was already showing the slight signs of the baby inside. Andrew beamed at her. He knew this journey would be dangerous, but they had to go, and he couldn't be happier than to be going with her.

Avery walked up to his horse, checking the cinch one more time, and then stepped up into the saddle, roughly shifting the saddle sideways to straighten it. He stood in the stirrups, working the slack in his pants down, and settled back into his seat. He rubbed at his eyes for a moment and then stood straight in his saddle.

"Well, ain't nothing stopping us but the leaving of it all. Andrew, you and ole Duke can take the first lead."

Andrew nodded and flicked his heels against Duke's flanks and they surged forward, their pack horse in tow. Kaya looked at Avery and he smiled, motioning her forward.

"After you, prego!"

He laughed and Kaya stuck out her tongue. She straightened herself, set her shoulders back, and had to merely lift the reins and Bonnie was off, eager to catch up. Avery glanced back once more at his home--the place where he and his father had been born. He took a deep breath and kicked his horse up.

"Avery?" called Kaya.

"Yes ma'am?"

"Are you really going to pack that guitar with you clear to South America?"

"I sure am. I'd starve before I left this thing. It's a family heirloom. Not only is it an original 1964 Gibson Dove, but it is also signed by none other than the king himself."

"Elvis?" She asked.

"What?! Hell no! King George. The king of broken hearts. I'd sing you one of his songs, but right now I'm in the mood for a good travelin' song."

Kaya laughed to herself, having no clue what he was talking about. She was about to ask when he started singing. It was the same song he had sung for them the night they made it to the ranch. She smiled at the memory of her and

Andrew swinging round and round. Her hand unconsciously rested on her stomach.

Andrew laughed hearing Avery belt out the song, but before long he and Kaya were both singing along, on the trail to Tierra del Fuego.

A NOTE FROM THE AUTHOR

Dear Reader,

I hope you enjoyed Wayward Prey. As my first novel, it is my baby. The spark for this story lit my imagination and has started me down a path of writing I never expected.

If you enjoyed the story, I humbly ask you to leave a review where you purchased the book. Reviews are the driving force that puts books in front of potential readers and are crucial for the success of a novel.

Also, if you'd like to know more about me and my other books, including the sequel to Wayward Prey, please visit www.PLSmithBooks.com and subscribe to the site.

Thank you,

P. L. Smith

ABOUT THE AUTHOR

P.L. Smith was raised on his parents' farm in the deserts of Northern Nevada. As a young adult, he was unsatisfied with the seclusion of farm life, so he struck out and traveled in his early twenties to explore the world. From China to Chile he gained experiences and memories that will stick with him forever. As happens to most vagabonds, eventually he met someone, put his passport away, and settled down.

Before long, kids came into the picture and he embarked on his most challenging and epic adventure yet—becoming a stay-at-home dad. Ironically he also returned to farming. He and his family bought a small farm in northern California, where there is plenty of space to play and plenty of juicy peaches to eat.

P.L. Smith wrote his first novel—Wayward Prey—amidst a break in his early travels. It was an accident really that he stumbled upon fiction writing. During a particularly tough time, he began journaling to alleviate the stress of the circumstances. Out of nowhere the story of a young boy running for his life began pouring out of him. After a month of writing the rough draft was complete. Followed by months of editing and a successful Kickstarter campaign the book was finally published. Soon he had a sequel mapped out and an entirely new fantasy series whose first book—The Firejack War was the next to be published. Shortly afterward life got in the way as it tends to do and adult-like responsibilities took priority. Writing is like going to the gym if you're not disciplined it is easy to fall off the wagon and the longer you go the harder it is to climb back on. Nearly a decade passed before he managed to complete another manuscript but thanks to an event called NaNoWriMo he felt inspired to test the waters again and jumped in with both feet.

His newest books—Scattered Prey (sequel to Wayward Prey) and The Dead Author Book Club are scheduled to be released sometime in 2024.

If you're interested in his writings he would love for you to tag along!

facebook.com/plsmithbooks

instagram.com/farmdadpoet